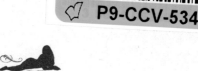

A King Production presents...

Ride Wit' Me 2

A Novel

JOY DEJA KING

ISBN 13: 978-0986004568
ISBN 10: 0986004561
Cover concept by Joy Deja King

Library of Congress Cataloging-in-Publication Data;
A King Production
Ride Wit' Me Part 2/by Joy Deja King, Royce Johnson
For complete Library of Congress Copyright info visit;
www.joydejaking.com
Twitter @joydejaking

A KING PRODUCTION

A King Production
P.O. Box 912, Collierville, TN 38027

A King Production and the above portrayal logo are trademarks of A King Production LLC

This Book is Dedicated To My:

Family, Readers, and Supporters.
I LOVE you guys so much. Please believe
that!!

—Joy Deja King

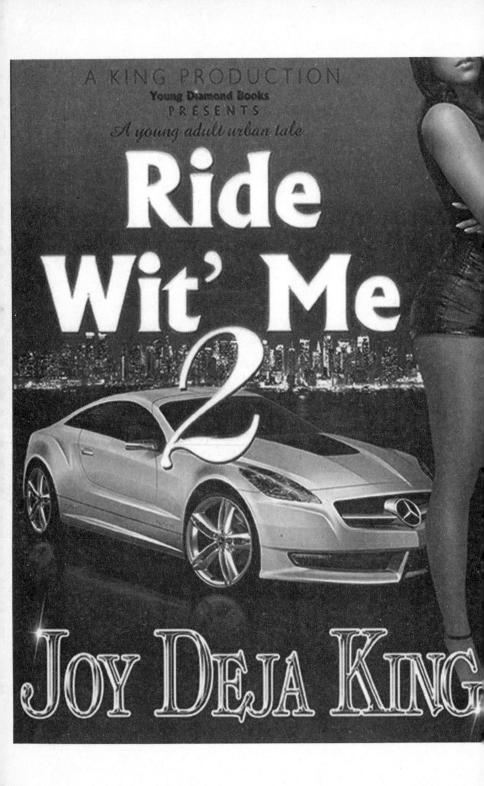

A KING PRODUCTION

Young Diamond Books

P R E S E N T S

A young adult urban tale

Ride
Wit' Me
2

JOY DEJA KING

Prologue

My Five Sons

"I called them one by one from the street corners, the bars, the dingy apartments in the Chicago projects. Come. Follow me. Be part of something bigger than the futile scramble for survival in the ghetto. Experience abundant life. Not in some nebulous place at some indistinct time in the future. Live abundant in the here and now. Wealth. Power. Not just for those who think they rule the world. But for us, my people.

Ronald Clinton was the first of my sons. Firm like the earth. Rumbles like an earthquake. Then came Richard Stones. Silent. Stealthy. Dispenser of swift retribution. And then my other sons. Adam Powers. Angry like a hurricane. Isaiah Jones. Intelligent, far-sighted. Laid-back soul brother. Dalvin Dewitt, wild like a fire. Savage. Furious.

I established the five points of my star on the foundation of my five sons—Earth, Spirit, Water, Air, and Fire. And then the others poured in from all parts of Chicago and beyond. Who am I... I am The Shepard.

Chapter One

Back In Your Arms

The gunshots felt like explosions going off inside my body. The world blazed into white light that sucked all the sound and feeling out of me and flung me forward like a dry leaf. Imagine what it's like to have a stick of dynamite go off in your back pocket.

I didn't know when I hit the sidewalk. Don't remember springing to my feet and turning to face him. But I remember the look on his face when I dragged the ski mask from his head. He had that wild look in his eyes, like he was seeing someone return from the grave. Didn't even try to defend himself when I swung at him. Just stood there.

I didn't feel my arms they were swinging like they were on autopilot. I saw him go down, saw the sidewalk float up to meet my face, soft and silent.

I heard the pain rush towards me from far away, and when it surged through me like a blazing ball of fire I wanted to scream like a girl. But I couldn't open my mouth. Couldn't move.

They came from all directions. All I could see were their shoes. Then I drifted into darkness.

I floated in and out of consciousness several times after that. Each time I rose to the surface the first thing I'd remember is the look in Jacob's eyes. I had seen it many times. That's how men look at you when they begging for their lives. His eyes seemed to burn into mine before melting into the darkness as I succumbed to the heavy sedatives pumped into me through the IV tubes.

My moms and Mercedes, my wife-to-be, practically camped out beside my bed in the hospital. Sweet Mercedes. The look of love and fear I saw in her wide-open eyes broke my heart. Why'd she have to witness this so soon?

Sometimes when I glided up from a blank, drug-induced unconsciousness, I'd see my dad hovering over me, his eyes sharp and piercing, his face hard and murderous. Once, when the nurse had left the room and we were alone, he leaned close to my ear.

"Who did this?" he whispered fiercely. "Who did this to you, son?"

But I couldn't speak. I couldn't tell him, although Jacob's name burned on my tongue.

"Whoever did this is a dead man," he vowed,

his voice an echo in the darkness that swallowed me like a wave.

Then one day I awoke. The room was dim and quiet except for a beeping sound that came from the machine and the soft rhythm of someone breathing. I turned my head. Mercedes was asleep in a chair beside my bed, her hand resting on my arm. I whispered her name, but she didn't hear me. I cleared my throat and tried again. She stirred.

"Mercedes," I forced the words between dry lips. "Baby, wake up."

She opened her eyes. The joy on her face was the purest I'd ever seen. I was alive. I came back, if only for Mercedes.

✧ ✧ ✧

THE STREETS SEEM DIFFERENT from before. They're colder. Meaner. Or maybe I'm the one that's changed. Although I've been out the hospital for five months this is my first day back hitting the pavement. The pain is still fresh from the bullets. I pump up on oxycodone every day and walk with a cane, but that hasn't altered my swagger.

My eyes slide from left to right, tracking every shadow of movement. My main objective was to find Jacob and rain down the retribution due to him. The lowlife ran off just before the ambulance came, and it seems like he's dropped off the face of the earth. People can disappear, but they can't vanish. He was somewhere and I would find him. But first things first. I have to re-establish my presence in the old neighborhood my territory since I was 15.

I felt my brush with death had rewarded me with razor sharp sight and hearing and a kind of extra-sensory perception. I welcomed it because I would need that and more if I wanted to eventually take over for my father and reign supreme over these streets.

Everyone in the hood knows me and welcomes me back. As I acknowledge the love by embracing a young blood, or stopping to say a few words to someone's mother, I sense the fear that lies at the heart of their loyalty.

"YO, DOG," SAYS MY boy Demetrius to Stephano. "I think she likes you, though. You don't think she likes you?"

Stephano snaps up his shoulders in a shrug. "Yeah, she likes me," he says. "But I don't roll wit chicks that age, y'know."

Stephano was from Cuba. I was intrigued to learn that his grandfather had been part of the revolution over there, and that he came from a family of street soldiers. He was older than me by about five years, didn't smile much, and don't felt no sympathy for men in pain or women in tears.

"Me?" he says to Demetrius, "I like my women

a lot older. Personally, I prefer her mother."

"Her mother?" Jimmy said. He was a New Yorker who did time in Rikers for slamming a guy through a plate glass window. "What about her sister?"

"Man," said Stephano, "her mother look just like her sister."

As they went back and forth with the small talk, I took the opportunity to speed-dial my girl.

"Hi, baby!" she answered sounding excited.

"You got my gift?" I ask.

"Yeah!" Mercedes squealed like a little girl. "I got it."

"You like it?"

"I love it!"

"You put it on?"

"Oh yeah, I got it on, and Keisha's eyes are just poppin' out of her head, ain't they, Keisha?" I hear her cousin say something in the background, and Mercedes laughs.

"Baby, I'm coming over to see you this evening," I say.

"I wanna see you too," she purrs. "I miss you."

"I miss you too, baby."

"I love you." Hearing Mercedes say those three words never got old to me. It was as if it breathed life into me, now more than ever.

"Love you too," I said and end the call.

I NOTICE THIS GUY STANDING OUTSIDE the diner who looks like a lawyer. Clean-shaven. Tailored suit. Slick. He eyes me up and down.

"That him?" I ask Demetrius.

"Yeah." He nods.

My boys and me walk up to him like a menacing human wall me and Demetrius in the center, Jimmy and Stephano flanking us on either side. Most men are intimidated by this formation, but if he was feeling threatened, he didn't let it show.

"What up, Spider," I said in a calm but stern tone.

"Hello, Dalvin," he replied in an equally cool tone.

We shake hands. Demetrius pushes open the door and stands aside, holding it open as I walk in. Spider enters after me and the others follow. It's warm in the diner, and we shrug off our coats as we stroll inside. The owner has been doing business with my father for years. Consequently, he lives in peace.

As we settle into a side booth, Demetrius reaches for two menus. He slides one in front of me and flips open his own.

"Yo, yo, yo, wassup, homies?" The owner's son, a second-generation Asian-American, bustles up to the table. He stretches out his fist to me for a pound, pulls out his little pad and fixes his eyes expectantly on me. I glance at Demetrius.

"Okay," says Demetrius, inclining his head in my direction, "so my boy is gonna have a BBQ bacon burger with fries, and I'll have a double cheese-burger with onion rings. Oh, and Dave... make sure my boy gets some extra sauce with them fries."

"Sure thing," says Dave, scribbling the orders on his pad.

See, Demi, he feels me. He knows what's in my head. Stephano's got my back, and Jimmy's my wing man. This is my inner circle. Nobody gets to me without going through them.

I turn my attention to Spider.

"I hear you the best," I say, looking him dead in the eyes.

"I am the best," he says.

"And your specialty is surveillance," I want to confirm.

"More than that," he responds. "Primarily, I'm in the information business, and I can get you what you want, when you want it."

"Oh?" I say, intrigued. I take a sip of the Coke Dave places in front of me.

"Say, for example, you want a company's assets. Or its money. I can get it for you. Or say you want information 'bout new weapons. Or new pharmaceutical research. Or new drugs. I can get you the information and the merchandise. Or if you want information 'bout people. Want to know their social security numbers, or their medical histories, or information 'bout their families or their sex lives. I can get you that information, and sell it for you to the highest bidder."

I don't answer immediately. I wanna savor the adrenaline rush. Dave places steaming plates in front of everyone. I sample one of my fries as I continue to contemplate.

"Furthermore," Spider continues smugly, "I can penetrate any intrusion detection system or any firewall on any kind of network anywhere in the world, so you can help yourself to... well... anything. Any problem you got, I can help you solve it."

"So how would you find the man I'm looking for?" I ask, dipping some fries into the sauce. There was no doubt that everything Spider said was very enticing, but this was about locating one person, the other stuff could wait.

Spider takes a bite out of his cheeseburger, and it seems like he's chewing on my question as well as his food.

"GPS," he says, swallowing. "It's everywhere now."

"So you mean I can just punch in his number and get his location?" I ask.

"Well, if it was that simple, you could do it yourself."

Huh! Cocky and not even trying to hide it I thought. "How soon can you find him?" I question, deciding to keep it cool.

"Gimme a few days," he offers. "You'll get your man."

I rest my chin on my knuckles and study him. He's a few years older than me. I make him out to be maybe 21, 22, tall, dark-skinned. Shrewd. Composed. His face a mask. I close my eyes and stroke my chin, allowing my instinct to do its thing. I open my eyes just as he glances at me, his face expressive for an unguarded moment before he slips the mask into place again.

"So what info you need to start?" I ask, smiling at how much his face had just told me.

Spider wipes his fingers with his napkin and tosses it onto his empty plate. "All I need is his name," he says.

"His name," I say, blinking away the image of the sidewalk floating up to meet my face, brushing aside the memory of Mercedes' torn dress and fearful eyes, swallowing the hatred coiling through me, "is Jacob Powers."

I PUSH MYSELF UP with my cane. It doesn't hurt so long as I take the meds, but the cold weather sometimes makes me feel stiff. Spider had left some time ago, and I saunter through the diner with my boys following a little ways behind. I walk with a limp now, which I cover up with a little bop that Mercedes says makes me look sexy. Dave's father comes from behind the cash register. He looks at me and bows slightly, indicating the door to his office, cause it's the fifteenth of the month. Pay day.

Chapter Two

Here Comes The Bride

I couldn't take my eyes off the diamonds that sparkled in the bracelet Dalvin had given me. I had never seen anything so beautiful, and I never thought I could feel sexy just from wearing a bracelet. It must have cost five G's or more. With all we had been through, the love was still there and it seemed stronger and even more powerful.

I sat cross-legged and flip the pages of one of the wedding magazines scattered over my bed. My eyes settle on a jaw-dropping, off-the-shoulder gown with an endless amount of rhinestones flowing down the side.

"Oh wow! I can see myself in this, how beautiful my skin would look against the ivory satin," I beamed out loud, imagining my wedding day.

I leap off the bed and spin round in the center

of my room with my arm stretched out, so the light can catch the rocks in the bracelet.

My mother taps at my door. I know it's her, because she doesn't knock, just taps with her nails. I dance over to the door and open it, swinging my arm in front of her eyes so she can see the sparklers up close. She snaps back her head and squints at the bracelet.

"D gave it to me," I sing.

"Nice." She smiles.

I can't tell if she's admiring it or being sarcastic, but I'm so happy, I don't care.

"You're everything that I dream about," I chant, still spinning, "talk about and brag about..."

She glides into the room and sits on my bed, pulling the folds of her negligee around her, crossing one leg over the other. My mom hovers a lot these days, always watching me. She's been like that since Dalvin got shot last year. She worries about me, and though I know it comes from a good place, it just annoys me especially lately. It's like she thinks I don't know what I'm doing, like she didn't make the same choices as me.

I see her eyes roam along my legs, which look toned and shapely in my hoochie shorts, and my breasts, round and perky in my sports bra. She tries on a little smile, but her face wouldn't have it. The corners of her lips curve down and her whole face collapses. I stop dancing and just look at her.

"Come here, Mercedes," she says in her soft,

husky voice. She pats the space on the bed beside her. "Come let momma talk to you."

I sigh and plunk down on the bed next to her. She reaches for my hand. Her fingers feel small and delicate.

"Sugarplum," she says, "I love you..."

"I know, mom−"

"Shhh..." she places a finger over my lips. I roll my eyes.

"...and I want you to be happy..." n

"I'm happy!" I wail. "You can't see I'm happy?"

She tries the smile again, and this time it sticks—a little stretch of the lips painted on to her face perfectly made up as if she going somewhere, which she ain't.

"...but you the only child I got, and I don't wanna lose you. I want you to be safe."

"How can I not be safe with Daddy's goons following me about everywhere?" I growl.

Since the attack on Dalvin, my father had insisted on having two men escort me everywhere I went. Usually, his soldiers shadow me so I don't know they're there, but these two were right up beside me. In the beginning, I had fun making them follow me around in circles and ditching them when they got good and confused. Then my dad threatened to ground me for good if I didn't stop doing that. It took months of persuasion, pleading, and open rebellion to get him to give me a little breathing space.

Her eyes slide over the magazines on my bed, resting on the open page that flaunts the breathtaking gown. She cocks her head and picks up the magazine, placing it on her knee. As her eyes devour the dress, her face softens, melts into a real smile. She looks up, not at anything in particular, as if she's seeing something far away.

"I remember when your daddy and me tied the knot," she murmurs. "Man, he threw a bash!" she laughs.

"Tell me about it, Ma," I say, taking advantage of this good sign.

She continues to look into the mist of time, her face a little bright, a little sad.

"Well, you know your daddy's well-connected," she says, smiling through the gloom that always clouds her face now. "Everyone and their momma was there. We did it at the Blood of the Lamb Baptist Church. Afterwards, we had a huge party at the Hilton. The cake was seven layers high and liquor was flowing like the Mississippi River. Oooh-man! I don't think there was a bash like that in those parts since. And Ronnie was such a hunk. Still is."

"And he still loves you," I say, touched by the sadness in her voice.

"Yeah," she says, nodding. "My baby still loves me."

"Did he ever cheat on you, Ma?" I ask, biting the bullet.

She chuckles at that, but doesn't answer.

"Okay," I say, "forget that. But y'all still together throughout everything. You don't think it could be that way for Dalvin and me?"

She doesn't answer immediately, as if she's rolling the idea round in her mind. She bends her head to gaze at the fabulous gown in the magazine on her knee.

"This really is a nice dress," she admits.

"Ain't it, though?" I say. "Man, I would look so fly in a dress like that."

"You sure would," she says, flipping the page. I snuggle close to her to get a better view of the glossy pages.

"Woah." She sighs, pausing at a picture of a skinny model in a strapless silk sheath. "Would you look at that?"

"Oooh!" I say in a rush of excitement. "Look at this one."

I snatch one of the magazines from the bed and flip the pages till I come to a strapless lace gown with a flowing train.

"That's the one I like," I say, poking the page.

"Gorgeous!" She breathes. She looks at me solemnly, then reaches out and caresses my face.

"Did he ask you yet?" she says.

"Not yet," I say.

"Try not to get your hopes up..."

"He's gonna ask, Mom. We talk about it all the time."

She holds my chin in her hand, and I see the tears brim over the corners of her eyes. Oh no, no, no, Ma. Not the waterworks again.

"Come," she says, brushing the magazine off her lap and rising from the bed. She grabs my hand and pulls me up as she makes for the door. I trail after her down the hall, into the room she shares with my dad.

When I was little, I used to think of this room as a magic room. To me, it was huge like a castle in a fairy tale and filled with so many secret places I could play hide and seek and never get found. Now that I feel grown and in my mind about to be married, I notice all the little things my parents did to make it a cozy nest just for them.

There's an enormous quilt hung up behind the king-sized bed that my mom says traces our family history from down south. I remember how I loved to climb up on the headboard and run my fingers over the patterns. Then I would dive into the bed squealing and giggling while my daddy pretended to be a grizzly bear searching for me among the pillows and spreads.

I love how they arranged the wingback chairs around the little table where they have their coffee in the morning, and how they have their favorite art and photos on the walls and bunches of flowers everywhere, and how the chandelier hanging from the high ceiling makes everything look sparkly and kind of magical.

We maneuver round the chairs and the statue of a black lioness pawing the air and head for the walk-in closet. My mom slides her arms out of her dressing gown, letting it slip to the floor and kicks off her furry slippers. As she strides ahead of me in her silk nightie I notice she still has a tiny waist and a curvy butt that glides with the smooth sway of her hips. God, I hope I look that good when I get old.

She opens the double door in a sweeping motion, flicks on the light and heads towards the back of the closet. Tapping her chin, she bends over to peer into the bottom shelf. Then she leans forward and tugs at a large trunk.

"Here, baby," she says, "help me with this."

I grab one of the trunk's handles and together we haul it out. She kneels down and lifts the lid, carefully peeling away a layer of delicate tissue paper. Inside are two of the most beautiful pillows I ever seen. She removes one of them and buries her face in it.

"Oh, ma!" I say.

I reach into the trunk and pull out the matching pillow, which is made of fine ivory linen and embroidered with hundreds of tiny pink roses.

"This is so pretty!" I press my face to it as I had seen her do and inhale the pillow's sweet rose fragrance. "Where'd you get this?"

"This," she says running her hand along the chest, "is called a trousseau. It's a collection of all the beautiful things you put together for your wedding."

"Oooh, Ma," is all I can say. I never heard of a trousseau before. It occurs to me that my mom is letting me in on something special, probably something she never shared with anyone else.

She places the pillow carefully aside and reaches into the trunk, pulling out a dainty little lace dress. She stands up and holds the dress in front of her, letting the skirt dance elegantly about her thighs.

"Wow!" I say. "Is that your wedding dress?"

"Goodness, no!" she squeals. "I wore this the day your daddy and me went off on our honeymoon. Oh yeah, baby. We did the whole nine."

I reach for the pretty dress and hold it in front of me.

"This is so cute!" I say, giggling with excitement.

She holds out a pair of silver satin shoes with wicked four-inch heels.

"I wore it with these," she says.

"Ma!" I say, slipping the shoes on my feet. "You were banging back in the day!"

She chuckles as she pulls out a black velvet box. She opens it and carefully lifts out a champagne glass with the letter "L" engraved on it. She holds it up and the light shimmers on its amber surface. She holds it out to me and reaches into the box, pulling out an identical glass engraved with the letter "R".

"Matching champagne glasses," she says. "Your daddy and me had the first drink of our married lives in these."

"Wow, how romantic."

She digs into the trunk pulling out more pretty dresses, a fabulously embroidered bedspread, a jewelry box. Then she pulls out a huge bundle of tissue and slowly peels it open.

She lets the tissue float out of her hands to reveal a dazzling bustier covered with white lace decorated with clusters of flower-buds. The train, wave upon wave of embroidered silk studded with multi-colored stones cascades to the floor. She holds the gown in front of me, lovingly arranging the fine fabric around my feet.

"Oh!" I whisper, close to tears. "Ma... it's beautiful."

She looks me over, nodding in satisfaction. "I married your daddy in this," she says softly.

She takes my hand and leads me to the mirror. My skin glows against the pretty lace. The floor around our feet is covered with the gown's glittering train and my mom's classy stuff. My new diamond bracelet flashes on my wrist. I feel like a fairy in a sparkling cloud. My face shines with the amazement I feel.

My mom stares at me with pride on her face, with a great big smile and looking young and pretty. She takes a bundle of my hair and winds it between her fingers, pulling it into a loose coil on top my head.

"Ooooooohh." She sighs. "Honey, you're beautiful. Truly beautiful. Would you like to be married in this gown?"

"Oh, Ma," I say. "I'd look like... a princess. I would. I would love to be married in this gown."

She nods, tugging at the waist. "Then it's yours. We may need to make a few alterations, though, cause you're a little tinier than me."

I hear the bedroom door slam. "Latoya...?" calls my father. "You in here?"

"Gimme a minute," yells my mom, hastily folding up the gown, and putting the gorgeous things back in the trunk. "Go talk to your daddy," she says, "and not a word about this. To anyone. Especially not to D. Not yet."

I stroll into my parents' room, feeling like I'd just stepped through a magic mirror. My father had turned on the flat screen TV and was standing in front of it, feet planted firmly on the ground, surfing the news channels.

"Oh, princess," he says, stretching out his arm as if he would scoop me into a hug though his eyes are glued to the screen. "You the one I wanna see."

I roll my eyes. What now?

"How the college applications going?" he asks absently, arm still stretched out, peering at the television.

"Good," I say brightly, skipping towards the

door. As I slip past him, I hear the news announcer say something about some dude getting smoked behind a school.

"I can't believe it," I hear him mutter as I swing out of the room into the hallway. "That's just how Shepherd used to do it."

WHEN I HEAR THE rhythm of Dalvin's cane echoing through the foyer I run down the stairs and fly into his arms just as he hands his coat and cane to Lillian. He staggers a bit from the impact of my one-hundred-and-twenty-five pound frame slamming into him, then he wraps his arms around me and swings me off the ground. He slips his tongue between my lips and squeezes me tight and I go all woozy just like it's the first time. I can't get enough of him. I want the moment to last forever. Then he releases me. I hold out the hand with the bracelet, and he takes it like a true gentleman would.

"I like your bracelet, miss," he says, eyeing my wrist.

"Ain't it hot?" I giggle. "My man gave it to me."

"Your man gave you that?" he replies coyly. "Wow! He must think you real special to lay that kind of bling on you."

"Course I'm special," I say, pulling him into the house. "You hungry? Want something to eat?"

"Sure," he says, following me through the living room into the kitchen.

"Healthy or junk?" I ask, going to the fridge.

"Junk, of course," he says, easing onto a stool by the island. I pull a pecan cake out of the fridge and balance it on one hand while I flip open the cupboard, lift out two plates, and take them over to him.

"Lemme help you with that," he says, rising from the stool.

"Nope," I say. "You sit right there. I got this."

I cut two big slices of the cake, placing them on the plates, aware of his eyes roaming over my body. I push one in front of him and lick my fingers. Then I go back to the fridge for two smoothies and put them beside the plates. He cracks the top off one of the smoothies and puts it to his lips.

"So how my baby doin'?" he asks.

"Okay." I pout.

"Whoah!" he says, smiling and digging into his cake. "What's that all about?"

"Nothing."

"C'mon," he pries, "what's going on? Daddy on your case again?"

"Goodness! He never eases up."

"He wants the best for you, y'know."

"D," I say, "whose side are you on?"

"Baby, I'm on your side... always," he assures me. "But I know how your dad feels. He worries about you. I worry about you too."

"Oh, please!" I said, getting annoyed. "It's always about school, school, school. And I'm sick of being followed everywhere I go."

"Speaking of school," D interjects, "how's it going with the applications?"

"Oh. My. Gosh." I scream. "You sound just like him."

Dalvin laughs. "Well I'm your daddy too, you know." He grins.

"Is that a fact?" I smile.

"I'm not?" he asks. I couldn't tell if he was serious or joking.

"Well, all that means is that I have to break you in just like I did him." I shrug.

"Really?"

"Uh-huh," I continue smiling as I toss my head. "I'll have to wrap you round my little finger. My other little finger."

"You have your daddy wrapped around your little finger?"

"Sure I do," I boast. "Can't you tell?"

He don't say nothing to that, just looks at me, with a slight grin.

I swear there wasn't another guy walking this earth as cute as D. He's tall and his body is slim and athletic. He was handsome with a slight hint of prettiness that he inherited from his mother since he looked just like her. He had her hazel-green eyes and smooth, narrow face. I also knew he had a dark side, but he was sweet, gentle and warm when we were together.

"Matter of fact," I continue, cutting a teeny piece of cake with my fork, "the applications are going pretty good. I'm applying to schools here and out of state too."

"Really?" Dalvin nods his head, sounding even more like my father. "Like where?"

"Like MIT, UCLA, NYU, and Yale," I say confidently. "I applied to the U of Chicago as well, and Loyola."

"That's real good, Mercedes," he says proudly. "You so smart any of those schools would be glad to accept you. You know I'll support you wherever you choose to go."

"Yeah," I smile, thinking about my mother's trousseau.

"What?"

"Nothing," I say, shaking my head and looking at my plate.

"Mercy." He pauses. I love when he calls me that. It's a nickname he gave me after he got out of the hospital. He says it kind of soft, as if the word means something to him. He lifts my chin and I look into his eyes again. "What's on your mind, baby?"

"It's... it's my mom."

"What about her?"

"Y'know, my moms, she got everything, but she ain't got a life."

Dalvin nodded his head.

"I mean, she really does not lack for anything. Daddy gives her the world. I don't even think he cheats on her. But you know, she don't have any friends, don't go anywhere, really. And she's sad all the time and cries a lot."

"Hmmm." He moaned as if in deep thought.

"It's because that's how he wants it. He don't want her to have anything but him. He just wants her entire world to be about him, and that's what she did made him her entire world."

He nods, frowning a little.

"I love my moms." I sigh. "She real sweet, you know? But I'm not gonna be like her. I'm not gonna let my father control my life." I look at Dalvin. "I'm not gonna let any man control my life. Not my father. Not my husband either."

He glances at me with a strange look on his face.

"Mercy, I ain't tryna control you."

Yeah, right. Where'd I hear that before? That's all men ever wanna do. Control women. That's what every man I've ever known has ever wanted to do. I didn't wanna argue with D so I didn't say anything. I got up and gathered the plates and forks and took them over to the sink.

"I wish summer would hurry up and get here so we can be married and move in together." As soon as I said it, my hand flew to my mouth. I felt embarrassed that I said that out loud. He chuckled a bit.

"Yeah, I want that too. More than anything."

"Today my mom wanted to know if you asked me to marry you. We always talk about it, but you never actually did. Ask, I mean. Properly."

"I know," he said putting his head down for a moment.

"Why?"

"Cause I wanna do it the right way," he says.

"What's the right way?" I ask.

"You'll see," he says, his smile lighting up his gorgeous eyes. He look so good, I feel I want him to make love to me right there in my dad's kitchen. I lean forward on my elbows and beckon to him in a naughty way with my finger to come closer. He leans in. I close my eyes and breathe deep as he kisses me.

Chapter Three

Enemies Surround Me

My nerves stayed on fire from the pain and the desire to destroy Dalvin Dewitt. But my dad didn't want me near him. We traveled slowly by car. What normally was a smooth three-hour trip by plane had been five months of pure torture. Not that it actually takes five months to make the trip by car, but we stopped every day for me to rest and take back roads instead of highways to cover our tracks.

Then there was the delay while I recovered from having my jaw and two of my ribs broken during the incident with Dalvin two months of non-stop pain. It hurt to breathe, it hurt to move. I had my jaw wired shut during that time, but even though the wires have been off a long time, it still hurts to open my mouth, and I'm famished all the time from not wanting to eat. But no matter how bad it is for me, I know it's worse for Dalvin. He lost a lung.

I can't help but wonder if what they say about his dad is true, that back when he was a young thug running the streets, he was shot five times at point blank range and lived. That's why they call him Bulletproof. Say that bullets can't kill him. That's what they say about Dalvin now. That he's bullet-proof like his dad. I mean, I used a .357 Magnum on him and he went down in a pool of blood. Then he just got up and came at me like the devil. I had never seen anything like it.

The crazy part is that it wasn't even about Mer-cedes. It was about Dalvin and me. He appeared suddenly outside my car that last night I went out with her. I didn't have time to react. That was the first time I'd really encountered him, though I'd been watching him for a long time. He was a sav-age. I couldn't fight him off. He won that round. But I don't believe in losing. My dad always says to win by any means necessary, like how he does. He says my enemies should never remain standing, be-cause if they're still standing, they've won. That's why I took a Magnum to him.

My dad came almost as soon as I called him, just before the ambulance. He was so angry I thought he was gonna kill me. Said I let Dalvin beat me twice. Called me a punk. But that wasn't the only reason he was mad. He didn't want me getting between him and Dalvin's father. We didn't go to the hospital. He called my uncle who's a surgeon, and he patched up my mouth and chest.

The night they burned our house to the ground, my dad, my uncle, and I, we just threw whatever we had with us into the truck and started driving. We move into a different hotel every week. And every night, we drive.

My dad is crazy. It wasn't so bad when he was away all the time on business trips and months would go by before I saw him. Now he's all over me. I always suspected he was a bit unhinged, obsessed with the past. Now I know for sure. He just won't let it go.

✡ ✡ ✡

THE TIGHT ARRANGEMENT OF CCTV cameras near the domicile of the client's fiancé provided me with pretty much everything I needed to know.

The client, the only son of a multi-millionaire crime boss in the city and heir to his father's empire, is actually under constant surveillance, as is his father, mother, girlfriend, future in-laws, extended family, employees, servants and everyone who even brushes shoulders with him in the street. Whether or not the client knows this isn't clear to me yet, though he wouldn't be worth his salt if he didn't.

I find crime families surprisingly casual about

the fact that their illegal projects and violent activities draw attention from the gatekeepers of the law almost from day one. Or maybe the reason for their over-confident attitude is that they think they're above the law because they pay so many public servants under the table.

From the sizable collection of images and data on record of the client and his associates, it's clear that the CPD, FBI, CID, CIA, IRS, DEA, Sheriff's Department, Homeland Security, etc. have had their eyes on that clan for a long time. You don't need to be a rocket scientist to figure out what they plan to do with all that intel.

I knew this the day I sat down to lunch with him and his soldiers. Dalvin Dewitt, or D, as he likes to be called, was an open book to me. As a matter of fact, I not only knew who he was, I also knew what he wanted to find the man who shot him. That man is Jacob Powers, currently a fugitive, location unknown but not for long.

The images of the attack are pretty clear. Client exits girlfriend's house and walks towards his convertible.

Target, aka Jacob Powers, steps out of parked car, advances towards client and drops him with a large-caliber weapon. Client springs up again, advancing towards target swinging.

Target goes down, as does client, who appears dead. Target crawls away from the scene like a wounded dog.

Client's girlfriend runs screaming from the house. Onlookers gather at the scene, obstructing clear vision of target from north angle.

East angle shows target crawling into his car, where he remains hidden. A red Toyota GT86 cruises up and double parks next to target's car. Target is helped into the Toyota by his father. Their escape is obscured by a gathering crowd.

Ambulance arrives on scene within minutes not surprising, given the impressive collection of wealthy families in that neighborhood.

Client is scooped off the sidewalk like an omelet and shoved into an ambulance on a gurney. Crying girlfriend climbs into ambulance.

I follow target's progress, skipping through a convenient web of CCTV cameras for several miles.

Toyota pulls up outside a steel and glass facility surrounded by barbed-wire walls. Target's father uses iris scan to enter facility with target. A quick zoom-in shows the name of the facility on a small steel plate beside the door. ALPAC Group International. Hmmmm.

Security network around facility is pretty advanced, even more than the Feds. Interesting. It's almost an hour before I get a feed from interior security cameras.

Three floors. Reinforced steel top to bottom. Cameras everywhere.

Ground floor. Row upon row of High-Mobility Multipurpose Wheeled Vehicles. VIP armored vehicles. SUVs. Sedans. Limos.

First floor. A maze of hallways and offices.

Second floor. An armory, bristling with weapons. Semi and fully automatic assault weapons. M-16s. M-4s. AK-47s. Bushmasters, Grenade launchers. A wide assortment of Rugers, Sig Sauers, Brownings, and Glocks. Shelves of ammo.

Target is laid out on a table in the midst of these weapons, in obvious pain.

One hour fifteen minutes later, another car pulls up outside facility. A man gets out and enters facility with iris scan. Goes straight to target's location and attends to target's wounds.

These people have enough fire-power to start their own war and win. Does Dalvin Dewitt know who he's stepping into?

✿ ✿ ✿

"EAT YOUR FOOD," my dad barks.

We're sitting at the dingy plastic dining table in the cheap motel room we're renting. It's hot in the room, and he had taken off his shirt. The tats on his chest and arms identify him as a gang member before he became an investment banker.

It's good southern soul food, but I can only pick at it. I don't wanna eat. The crazy look on Dalvin's face as he flew at me burns in my memory. Food settles like bile in my stomach. I ignore my father, which only makes him mad.

"Eat," he growls, jabbing his finger in my direction. "I don't want you complaining tonight about how you hungry."

He picks a piece of fried chicken from his plate and stuffs it in his mouth. I stick my fork in the food and ease a small piece of mashed potato between my teeth.

I hear the sound of the key turn in the lock. The door opens and my uncle walks in. He looks at me as he closes the door, his eyes cool and professional. He comes over and sits on the chair beside me.

"How you doing, Jacob?" he speaks softly, placing his thumbs under my eyes and pulling them down. "You not looking too good. How you feeling?"

"Sick," I mumble, nauseated. "Sick to my stomach."

"Stop your whining," my dad shouts, punching a number into the cheap cell phone he had picked up earlier that day.

"I been tryna get us a room in the next town, Adam," my uncle informs us.

"Me too," my dad shot back, "but I keep getting put on hold... Yeah..." he mumbles into the phone. "I'm trying to book a room for myself, my brother and my son... how hard is it to get a room in these hick towns? I don't care. I just want a room... a double room, yes, for me and my brother and my son...

one night only... my name is Jeffreys... yes, Carlton Jeffreys... yes, please do, and please don't put me on..."

He looks at me like it's my fault the person on the other end put him on hold. He ends the call and flings away the phone.

"Dad," I pause because it still hurts to talk, and my voice cracks. "Can we stay here a little longer? I can't take the driving anymore. My whole body hurts."

He looks at me, his eyes hard. "No," he belts. "We cannot stay here another night. You know the deal. And stop looking at me like that. I didn't tell you to go stepping into Dalvin."

"It'll take a little while more before you feel better," my uncle says, "but the pain will soon go away and you'll be fine."

"What did Shepherd say?" my dad asks my uncle.

"He say he don't want Jacob hurt," my uncle replies glancing over at me.

"See, Jacob," my dad says to me. "Shepherd don't want you to get hurt any more than you already are."

"But I don't wanna run."

"We ain't runnin," my dad hisses. "We taking you someplace safe. Look at yourself. You ain't in no condition to take on Dalvin Dewitt."

"I ain't a punk," I insist.

My dad stares at me, his eyes fierce. Then he

sighs and gets up from the table with his styrofoam plate. He still has a six-pack and he moves quickly towards the kitchenette.

"I'm sorry I said that," he says, crumpling up the plate and sticking it carefully into a garbage bag. "I know you ain't. I was angry."

I watch as he goes over to our bags stacked neatly by the door and picks up a black case. He brings it over to the table.

"You gotta use your head when you dealing with Dalvin," he says, sitting down and opening the case. He takes out his Sig Sauer. "I know that from experience. Something I been tryna teach you."

He pulls back the slide, slips it off the frame, takes off the spring and the barrel, and places them on the table.

"And you gotta see the bigger picture," he continued, cleaning the inside of the barrel. "It ain't only about you, okay? This is bigger than you."

I look down at my plate, anger boiling inside me. But I don't say anything else, cause I don't have the energy to argue with him.

"Here," my uncle says taking my plate, "lie down. I'll give you something to help you sleep a little before we go on the road again."

I go to the couch and stretch out my cramped body. My father reassembles the Sig.

"Don't worry bout Dalvin," he says to me. "He'll get his. He'll get his good. That's a promise."

He places a chair between the couch and the

door and sits in it, his face to the door, his Sig on his knee.

An image of Mercedes floats briefly before my eyes as I drift into sleep. On her back in my car. Eyes wide with terror. Lace bra showing through her torn dress. Me feeling like I'm about to explode even before I get my pants off, cause truth be told, I much prefer to take it by force than to have it served up on a platter, especially the spoiled, preppy types.

The memory of Mercedes screaming as I pin her down, her face streaming with tears, makes me smile.

✡✡✡

THEY CALL ME A hacker, a derogatory term I resent. Most of the breakthroughs in surveillance technology have been due to people in my profession, you know, and we keep pushing the envelope as far as the technology is concerned.

I prefer to think of myself as an innovator in the BOK of IT, developing new software, creating new viruses and providing a valuable service to anyone who can pay my fee and my services don't come cheap in this economy. My clients include celebrities, politicians, business people, and militants of every shade. I don't discriminate. Some assignments take months of careful planning, preparation, and execution. This assignment is still in the preliminary phase, because what I thought was gonna be a simple matter of tracking a missing man, is turning out to be much more complex and sinister.

I penetrate the intrusion detection network inside the facility and as I scan their folders, I discover files of blueprints for weapons and vehicles. Hmm. So they're also into R&D.

Lists of clients. Domestic clients. Foreign clients. UK. Australia. Iran. Africa. Looks like they're some kind of private military company. Mercenaries. Not nice people. Ooookay. Time to find out who's running this joint.

I scan the system for the principals of the company. President: Andrew Hawkes. Hawkes... Name rings a bell. I make a search for the really important folks. Shareholders. Investors. Why am I not surprised to see a familiar name on the list? Adam Powers, Vice-President, Investments, JD Bank. Councilman Adrian Powers. Dr. Stephen Powers.

Dalvin Dewitt, you've just upped your game, my brother.

Chapter Four

Unite And Conquer

You'd think that with all the vexation I face on the job I could at least find a little peace in my own home. But no. Vexation follows me right into my own house, in this case, Dalvin Dewitt, son of my former blood brother, Dalvin Dewitt Senior, who I haven't spoken to since we parted ways 15 years ago.

The first thing I see when I walk into my kitchen is him kissing my daughter on the lips. I send her packing upstairs to her mother.

I close the door to my study and pull out my chair, watching as he slides into a chair opposite my desk and settles into it, legs apart, soles of his feet on the ground.

Body language is important in our line of work. The way a man carries himself tells you whether he's soft or a real man. The boy is sure of himself. He looks me directly in the eye and waits for me to speak. I like that. Shows respect. Also shows he knows enough not to run his mouth, which could be the difference between living to see another day or dying in a hail of bullets cause you too stupid to know who you stepping into. I get to the point.

"Son, I know I said you could date my daughter, but I don't expect you to be getting physical with her under my roof. In fact, I don't expect you to be getting physical with her at all. If it happens again, you will not be welcome in my house."

He's calm. Doesn't bat an eye.

"I apologize, sir," he says. "I don't mean any disrespect to you or your household, and it won't happen again. Matter of fact, I'm glad to have this opportunity to speak with you."

"Oh yeah?" I ask. "Why?" I know the answer and don't wanna hear it.

"Because sir, I'd like to ask for your daughter's hand in marriage."

"Nah. That ain't gonna happen. He fixes me with a cool stare that makes him look like his daddy. It's clear he intends to battle it out with me. I could flip that chair with him in it and kick him out of my house, but then Mercedes would stop speaking to me again for sure. Wasn't worth it. Besides, I want to talk to him. Something about him had been bugging me for a long time.

"How you feeling?" I ask skipping over his

question.

I've broached a subject he doesn't want to talk about, and he takes his time before answering.

"I feel fine, sir," he assures me.

"Son." I bite down on my bottom lip, irritated that I have to explain this to him. "I been running the streets a long time. I seen men go down in a hail of bullets, including your father. I seen some of them stay dead, and some of them get up. The ones that get up, they lucky if they the same men they used to be. I know you lost a lung. So don't play wit me. I asked you how you feeling."

He looks at me, faintly amused. "I have good days and bad days," he says, shrugging.

I nod, knowing exactly what he means. I still have a piece of metal lodged in my right leg.

"Well, today's obviously a good day for you," I say. "Cause you smooching my daughter in my kitchen. How you figure that?"

He doesn't say anything just shifts his gaze slightly.

"Still doing therapy?" I question.

"Yes sir, and my doctor says I'll be fine. In fact, he says I can live a full and normal life even with one lung."

"Son." I briefly hesitate as I wonder if he actually believed what he just said. "They ain't nothing normal about your life."

There ain't nothing normal about Dalvin Dewitt. Gun runner. Drug Dealer. Just eighteen years old and already an enforcer with a taste for violence. Known for being merciless. Unpredictable. Even the Cobras think twice before messing with him.

Personally, I think he off-the-chain crazy. He would slam a man's head into a wall and crack open his skull then go eat burgers with his boys. Break a man's ribs with a tire iron then spend the next hour playing video games. To him there are no consequences for anything he does cause his father had spun a whole network of people around him whose only job is to shield him from consequences.

Now after getting shot by Adam Powers' son and surviving, he thinks he invincible. So does everyone else. Bulletproof. But I been running the streets long enough to know that no one ain't bullet proof. The bullet with his name on it ain't found him yet, that's all.

And that's exactly why I didn't want him near my Mercedes. I took pains to keep her away from the violence of our lifestyle, but his father steeped him in it like a teabag from the time he was small, grooming him to take his place. Now he's sitting in front of me looking like a mild-mannered altar boy, but I know who I'm dealing with. I know his mind. I know his soul. I bet I even know the dreams he dream at night, cause I'm him. And I been him longer than he been himself.

"I'm sorry," I tell him. "I can't let you marry my daughter. See, you're bad news. Trouble. I want

Mercedes to have a good life, with a husband who can give her the good life she deserves. What if she'd walked outta here that day with you? I would have lost my only child. Nah. Nah. I don't want that. I don't."

"So what do you want?" he asks. His eyes had gone stone cold. He's angry, but keeps it under control. "You want her to marry some corporate dude that don't know nothing about the life we live? You think I'm trouble? What about you? Her life has always been in danger just because she's your daughter. I know the danger that's all around her, and I can protect her from it just like you. Better than you."

I had to admit, he had a point about knowing the dangers surrounding Mercedes, but as for being able to take care of her better than me, he was way off.

"I would never do anything to put Mercedes in danger. I love her."

"Love?" I repeat before laughing. "What you know 'bout love? You think love is some nice feeling below the belly button? A little making out in the back seat of your car?"

"No sir. I do not think that. When you love a woman, you commit yourself to her, body, mind and soul. Forever. That's how I love your daughter. And she loves me."

"Then wait," I propose. "Wait a little. Give it time."

"Give what time?" He seems confused by my request.

"Give yourself time. Give her time to know what she really wants."

"We know what we want," he says with confidence, "like you knew what you wanted when you married your wife."

I wish they wouldn't go there. Things were different 17 years ago. Back then we had values. We did what we had to do, but we understood the difference between right and wrong, and we knew when we did wrong. Kids today got everything twisted. They think wrong is right and right is wrong. That's why the whole world's going to shambles.

"Mr. Clinton, I don't wanna go against your wishes. I wanna marry your daughter with your blessing. I'd like you to reconsider your decision."

"And if I don't?"

He doesn't answer, just gives me a cold stare that tells me he has every intention of getting his way.

"Here's the thing," I say. "I'll allow you to continue to date Mercedes. But I don't wanna hear nothing more about marriage, weddings, or anything like that. I want Mercedes to finish her education, maybe in a foreign country so she could see something of the world, grow up a little."

"I want that for her too," Dalvin concedes.

"Actually," I can't hide the irritation in my

voice, "you don't have any say in her life, and I'm not interested in what you think."

Dalvin is silent for a moment.

"Mercedes is her own woman," he says, coldly. "She not a minor anymore, you know. She can make her own decisions now, and if you force her to choose between you and me, you'll lose."

I couldn't believe the outright cockiness of this boy. The nerve. The audacity. I couldn't trust myself in the same room with him.

"Get out," I demanded.

✡ ✡ ✡

BUT HE'S RIGHT, I THOUGHT. Dead right. He had got up from that chair and walked out of the room without a backward glance. Last thing I heard was the front door slam.

I made up my mind that when I saw Mercedes later that night, I would tell her to forget all that stuff about love and marriage and focus on her education. I would choose a nice exclusive school for her to go to, someplace far from Dalvin, maybe in the UK, or even France or Switzerland like the white girls. What's the point of being rich if you can't lavish your children with the best that money can buy?

There were only a few people scattered along the benches in the park. A couple business people, cell phones to their ears, hurry through. In a few weeks it was going to be spring, and the parks were going to be filled with shrubs and flowers and kids playing. It wasn't so long ago that I was a young father in the park with my little girl. Where did the time go?

Although deep in my thoughts, I'm aware of his presence before I see him. Two suits stroll along the perimeter of the park to my right. I glance the other way. Another suit. Female. Out of the corner of my eye, I see his Rolls cruise by. Then I hear his long, unhurried stride. He hawks loudly, and his spit hits the concrete with a hard splat. I turn. Dalvin Dewitt, but this time not the son but the father is strolling towards me, hands buried in the pockets of his coat, collar pulled up against the February chill. He looks like a corporate executive. He's managed to stay trim and he still looks like a man in his prime.

I wasn't surprised to hear his voice on the phone. I had thought of calling him a few times, but something always got in the way. I was glad he beat me to it. Of the two of us, he was always the bigger man, except it wasn't exactly a social call. He wanted something, and I almost didn't keep our appointment. It was the conversation with his son that made up my mind.

"What up, blood?" He held out his hand. I take it, leaning in for the hug. I feel the pressure of his hand in my back, and I return the embrace. Just like the old days.

"Same ole, same ole," I say. "Mo' money, mo' trouble."

"I hear that," he says in agreement. "How's the family?"

"Good," I say, aware of the stiffness in my voice. "Yours?"

"Fine," he stares, eyeing me. "Looking good."

"I been hitting the gym," I add, offering him a cigarette. "Three times a week." I notice the mark on his hand and remind myself who I'm dealing with.

"Me too," he lets me know. "I'm not as disciplined as you, though." He snorts a puff of smoke out of his nostrils.

We strolled along together in silence for a while.

"What's on your mind, Dalvin?"

"Money," he says without hesitation.

"You don't have enough?" I question.

"Man, you can't never have enough." He laughs. I glance at him and he rolls his rattlesnake eyes in my direction.

"I'm working on a little project, like I told you. It could use your touch."

"Oh yeah?"

"You might also wanna use the opportunity to settle some old scores."

"I don't have old scores," I tell him. "When someone messes with me, I deal with them right away."

"Yeah, I know."

He puffs on his cigarette, deep in thought. I let him think.

"Times are changing, man," he says after a while.

"Got that right."

"And you gotta change right along with them."

"Agreed."

"And you gotta think of the future."

"True."

"The kind of future you gonna leave for your kids, y'know?"

"You ain't thinking 'bout world peace now, are you?"

Dalvin laughs. "Matter of fact, I'm thinking 'bout succession."

"Excuse me?" We reach the end of the park and turn, strolling in the opposite direction.

"Succession. Who gonna take over from me in the future?"

"That would be your son, right?" I flick away my cigarette.

"Yeah, definitely. He's a fine boy. A fearless soldier. Smart too. Good head for business. I gave him two of mine to run, and he's starting up one of his own now."

"Right..." my tone sounds unimpressed.

"Whassamatter? You don't like my son?" he sounds amused, like he's baiting me.

"You asked me here to pick a fight with me,

bro?"

"Just the opposite," he stops before continuing. "I want to extend an olive branch."

"For what?" I growl. "What's done is done. Years ago. It's over."

"I thought maybe we could bury the hatchet."

"You already buried it, Dalvin," I remind him. "In my skull. But you right. It is time to let bygones be bygones."

He coughs and throws his cigarette away.

"Our kids. They make a real cute couple, don't you think?"

"What you want from me, Dalvin?"

"Lighten up already, Ronnie, c'mon. Ease up the pressure a little."

"Your son put you up to this?"

"Nope."

"Then who did?"

"Nobody. Like I said, I've been thinking of the future. Life is short."

"What? You sick?"

He sighs deeply. "Let's just say there comes a time when you know you're not as invincible as you thought you were."

"So when did you figure that out, Bulletproof?" I laugh.

"When I saw my son dying in that hospital bed." He stops walking, and I pull up beside him. His face is creased with pain. "He was dying, Ronnie. Just like I was dying when I took five in the chest. Remember? I owe you my life, man."

"Forget it," I say, letting the dark memory just slide on out of my mind.

"I was by his side as he fought for his life. And by some miracle, he came back to me."

"Tell me something, you really believe you bulletproof? That bullets can't kill you?"

"Man no," he huffs. "But other people believe it, and that works for me. But getting back to our kids. My son wants to do right by your girl."

"Don't go there, Dalvin."

"Hear me out, Ronnie."

"Did he put you up to this? Tell me the truth, now."

"I swear, Ronnie. I never discussed this with him. But I know his mind. I know my son."

You and me both, bro.

"There are some things that are inevitable. Things you can't control."

"Like what?"

"Like time." Dalvin stares ahead of him. He starts to walk again, in a kind of absent way. "You can't control time," he says adamantly, "but you can control what you do while you're living in it."

"What's your point?"

"I want you to think ahead, Ronnie. I want you to think in terms of dynasty."

I roll this over in my mind, catching his drift.

"Like the white folks. Like the Jews. That's how they got so much power in this country. By intermarriage and creating dynasties that go on for generations, getting bigger and bigger. Our kids want to do it of their own free will. I consider that most fortuitous. Think of the wealth and power we'll amass if our families unite."

Wealth and power. He's speaking my language.

"So... you want me to give your son my blessing to marry my daughter? So we can expand our power base?"

"Significantly expand our power base," he says. "Expand our territory. Increase our resources. Besides, they young and in love. Remember them days?"

I laugh. "What you tryna do? Take me down memory lane?"

"Man," he says, "Latoya was fine back in the day. Every brother in the hood wanted to get wit her. She still fine. She ain't never gonna lose it, ain't she?"

"Nope," I say. "And after you couldn't get her, you went and married that uptown girl."

"Man, we were some high rollers back then."

"You can say that again, my brother." We reach the other end of the park and swing round again. "I spoke to him, you know."

"Who?"

"Your son Dalvin."

"Oh yeah?"

"He was at my house, tryna ask for my daughter's hand in marriage."

He laughs. "What'd I tell you? He's a fine boy. His mother brought him up right, you know."

"And what did his daddy do?"

"Taught him reality."

"Maybe too much."

"Nah. You can never have too much reality. If you'd done like me and had a son, you'd understand."

"She too... too young, Dalvin."

"No, she ain't. Back in the day girls was getting hitched way younger than her."

"That was then. This is now. Girls have so much more opportunities now. They can have... careers."

"So why can't she have a husband and a career?"

"Man, I don' know..."

"You just don't wanna let go of that girl."

"She growing up too fast, man."

"She already grown. You gotta let her go, Ronnie."

"I don't want this life for her, Dalvin."

"Well, I got news for you. She already living it. She was always living it, and everybody knew it but her."

"I... I..."

"Say it, Ronnie."

"Fear. Okay? I... fear for her life... She my little girl..."

"I got you..."

"Don't you feel that way about your son?"

"Sure, I do. And the way I dealt with it was to teach him street smarts, teach him how to fight and come out the winner. He tough. He can take care of himself. And he can take care of Mercedes too. Trust me on that one. Besides, we'd have an excuse to throw a party."

"Since when do we need an excuse to party?"

"I mean par-tay."

"Like it's 1999?"

"Man, you getting old," he says, laughing. "1999?"

"And our wives will like it too," I admit.

"They sure would," he agrees.

"Thank you," I finally said.

"For what?"

"For reaching out. I'm not big on forgiveness."

"I know. Me neither. Thank our kids for making it happen," he said. "I miss the old days. The way we used to roll together. The crazy things we used to get up to, man."

"Yeah, me too. But like I said, I have a little project in mind that you might like."

"What kinda project?" I asked.

"I wanna own this city." There was a harsh edge to his voice. "See all them Jews and Caucasians and Asians and all them rich folks? I want their money in my pocket. And see all them Italian and Japanese and Russian families that think they running things? I want them under my thumb."

"So how you gonna get that done?"

"I'm gonna run for mayor."

I stare at him.

"I want you to manage my campaign," Dalvin Senior offers without missing a beat.

Chapter Five

Ghost From The Past

"Come on, Mercedes," my mother called from the hallway. "How long you gonna stand in front that mirror?"

"Gimme a minute, Ma," I holler, taking a long look at myself. I was wearing some sexy black leather shorts and my thigh-high platform stiletto boots. I couldn't decide if I wanted to pair with my black leather jacket or my black suede jacket. Hmmm.

The leather was tight-fitting at the waist, with a diagonal zipper and ruffles at the sleeves. The suede was also tight-fitting too, with long flared cuffs, silver snaps, and a little flare at the hips. I put on the leather and twisted a bit to get a better view.

"Mercedes!" my mother called out again, but this time much louder.

"Coming!" I yelled back.

I pulled off the leather and tried on the suede. I zip it up and take a final look at myself. My hair is pulled up in a neat spiral on my head. I'm wearing hoop diamond earrings and the bracelet D gave me. I look hot, like Rihanna hot.

Since it wasn't so windy outside, I wasn't gonna wear my long fur-lined leather coat, but I couldn't decide if I should wear my fox fur.

"Mercedes!" my mother called out again, sounding annoyed. "Come on! We don't have all day."

"Okay, okay," I said, pulling on the fox fur and blowing myself a little kiss. I grab my purse and head out into the hallway.

My mom is downstairs in the foyer, her phone to her ear. As I clomp down the stairs, I see her eyes slide up over my outfit. When I reach the bottom, I spread my arms and do a little spin. She nods.

The limo is already waiting in the driveway. My mom pulls on a thigh-length black mink. Maurice, talking to invisible soldiers on his neat, little headset, opens the front door for my mother and me with the respect you'd show to royalty. We step outside. It's not terribly windy, but I stick my hands in the pockets of my coat to keep them a little warm.

Maurice goes to the limo and opens the door for my mother and she slips into the seat. He goes around and opens the other door for me and I get in. Then he goes around to sit beside the driver, and we pull out of the driveway.

MY MOM MOVES THROUGH the mall with a smooth, confident swagger. This is not your typical mall, like the ones I go to when I'm kicking it with my cousin Keisha. It's a luxury mall, and in here, most all the women wear minks and furs. But none of them don't have nothing on my mom's.

She walks through the mall like a queen wearing a black lace form-fitting dress under her mink. Her legs look shapely in a pair of black pantyhose and black platform shoes with wicked red high heels. She's wearing her hair loose, and it falls in honey-brown curls over her shoulders. She has a silk scarf over her hair and draped around her neck, and she got on a wide-brimmed hat over this tilted at an angle. Her style is haute couture with a bit of ghetto chic. Just wicked. I feel proud to be walking beside her like I'm her man. I can't help but laugh to myself at that thought.

She don't turn her head to look at herself in any glass or mirror, and she don't step aside to let anyone pass by. So as she strolls through, everyone else steps aside. My mom might be a softie when it comes to my dad, but she's a diva out of doors.

I notice that her eyes scan the mall. Though my dad has surrounded us with paid soldiers whose job is to make sure no one gets within ten feet of us, I guess she been married to him long enough to not take anything for granted.

As we swing into Neiman Marcus, I sneak a peek at one of the mirrors that cover the walls. My moms and me totally outclass everyone else in the shop. I feel myself holding my head a little higher and walking with a little extra bounce.

We're shopping for new stuff to wear to the big family dinner later that night to celebrate the reuniting of our families. The dinner was Mrs. Dewitt's idea. It was taking place at the Four Seasons. Moms and me were getting new gowns, shoes, accessories the works. After Neiman's, we were gonna hit Versace, Gucci, Vera Wang, and Tiffany's. The final stop on our glam tour was the salon.

The hostess escorts us through the restaurant, which looks big and bright from the sunlight pouring through the plate glass walls. It's warm inside, and the people at the tables all look like they've stepped out of *Vogue* and *GQ*. The hostess pulls out our chairs at our reserved table, and as we settle into them, tucking our big shopping bags out of the way under the table, a waiter pours sparkling water into our goblets.

Things have been happening so fast lately, I hardly have time to think. The most amazing thing was the complete change in my dad's attitude towards Dalvin and me. All of a sudden, like overnight, he went from hostile to happy. Well, not happy exactly, but as close to it as my dad will ever get.

He was real mad the day he walked in on me and Dalvin in the kitchen, and I thought he was gonna go psycho on me again. But he calls me into his room that night and sits me on the bed and starts talkin' bout how he gave a lot of thought to me and Dalvin, and how he's giving me his blessing for us to be married, and how he didn't mean to hurt me, but I'm his only little girl and he loves me so, so much and wants the best for me, yada, yada, yada. I swear at one point I thought I saw tears in his eyes.

"Dad," I say, reaching up and feeling his forehead. "You okay? I mean, you didn't fall down and bang your head or anything?"

He takes my hand from his forehead and puts it to his lips.

"No, baby girl," he says. "I'm fine. I... I'm sorry for being a selfish fool. Can you forgive me?"

"Of course I do, Daddy." My heart felt it would pop outta my chest from the happiness I felt. Of all the people in the world, I love my daddy the most. And I love my future husband with all my heart. And the thought of being able to have them both in my life without conflict was like being in heaven. Life couldn't get more perfect.

"I'll call Dalvin tomorrow and speak to him, okay?" he says sincerely.

"Okay, Daddy," I say, feeling more happy than I ever been in my life.

"Just promise me one thing, baby girl," he says, taking my face in his hands.

"Anything, Daddy."

"Promise me..." The look in his eyes is so intense, my heart skips a beat. "Promise me that if for any reason... any little reason at all... something don't feel right... in here..." he puts his hand on my gut. "If for any reason something don't feel right, you'll come to me?"

"I will."

"Promise you'll come to Daddy. Okay? Okay, baby?"

"Okay, Daddy. I promise." He hugs me so tight I can't breathe. Wow, how things change.

"CAN YOU BELIEVE IT?" I say to my mom, snapping out of my reminiscing back to the present. "What do you think changed his mind like that?"

"I don't know," she says and shrugs. I get the feeling she does know, but don't wanna tell me.

"Y'know, mom," I say, taking a sip of water. "Some day, you and Daddy gonna have to stop treating me like a little girl and start treating me like a grown woman."

She laughs a great big laugh that causes her to spill water on her dress.

"That's true," she says, continuing to laugh as if unable to control herself. "And that day is today, right?"

"Right."

"Well, okay, Miss Grown Woman." She giggles a little more. "The time has come to make some serious preparations."

"That's what's up."

"How do you feel?" she asks, spreading her napkin on her knee as the waiter puts our food on the table.

"Excited."

"A little scared, maybe?"

I think about this. "Ummm no." I shake my head.

"No?"

"No. But I feel as if... I'm about to leave my old life behind and move into my new life."

"I got you." My mom nods.

"So much new stuff going on." I smile. "New attitude from Daddy. New husband. New school. New clothes. Some nice new clothes too..."

"Yep. Nothing like new clothes..." Suddenly, her whole face freezes. Maurice appears out of nowhere and stands behind her chair. I could see the bulge of his hand gripping the butt of his gun under his coat. About five suits appear around our table, one of them standing directly behind me. My mother places her hand on mine, and I look around my heart pounding fast to see what's going on to disturb her and rile up my father's soldiers.

All I see is a fly young dude in a suit, feet planted wide apart, standing a little way from our table, his eyes on my mother.

"Excuse me, Mrs. Clinton," says eye candy, sounding like an Ivy League grad. "I apologize for interrupting your lunch. But my employer would welcome the pleasure of your company at his table."

My mom and me look in the direction of his stretched out arm. I see a man in a wheelchair sitting at a table a little way off, his back to us.

My moms sizes up the young dude. Her hand is still resting on mine, and she squeezes my fingers to let me know everything's alright.

"Who are you?" she asks, her voice cool. "And who you working for?"

The young dude's eyes shift from my mother to Maurice and the bulge under his coat, but he ain't worried.

"My name is Stones," he says, sliding his eyes towards me then back to my mother. "And my employer is an old friend."

My mom looks past Stones to the dude in the wheelchair, who had swung it around and was maneuvering around the tables heading in our direction. It's one of those automated chairs, and it makes a little whirring noise as he drives over. My moms looks at him, a puzzled look on her face. He's an ugly old dude, skinny and hunched over with a black patch where one of his eyes used to be.

I see her expression change to disbelief, then complete shock as the old dude gets a little closer to us. He stops beside Stones and swings his head from side to side as if he's sniffing the air. Maurice inches his hand out of his coat just enough to show the butt of his gun. My dad's soldiers step in a little closer to my mom and me, showing the butts of their guns too, looking like they ain't about to take no prisoners.

"Hello, Latoya," says the old dude, as if he's known my mom all her life. His voice is hoarse and gravelly, and he wheezes as he talks as if he can't get enough air.

"I don't mean to alarm you. But may I have the pleasure of your company for lunch?"

Moms don't answer. I get the feeling she too shocked to say anything.

"Please," says the old dude, sounding cool and casual, not like he begging at all. "I been waiting for this opportunity for a long time."

My mom nods slightly. "It's okay, Maurice," she says in a tense little voice. "I know this gentleman." She looks at Stones as if she's really taking in his features for the first time.

There are moments in your life that are like turning points, you know? That put you on a whole different path from the one you expected or dreamed about. You don't realize it at the time, because you just don't recognize the significance of those moments while you're caught up in them.

Maurice takes a step backward and the old dude drives up to the table. Stones steps back too and stands a little way behind the old man. I now know that that was the moment I stepped out of my old sheltered life into a new crazy dangerous life. I wasn't ready for that because it wasn't my choice. It was a choice that was made for me.

I squint my chair around a little closer to my mom, and she slides her hand down to my thigh, cause she can see I'm uncomfortable. The old dude parks his chair next to me. Stones moves forward and leans in to the old dude, who whispers something in his ear. Stones nods, then turns and walks off, leaving us alone.

The old dude is even uglier up close. Not only is he missing an eye, that whole side of his face is scarred, like if whoever had dug out his eye had ripped away his flesh as well.

His other eyeball is stuck in the corner of his eye, so you can't tell if he's looking at you or not. And though he's thin like a skeleton, his skin hangs off his bones.

But he's wearing a real nice suit, a felt hat on his bald head, a big gold ring on his finger, diamond studs in both ears and a nice, expensive cologne, and I get the feeling he wasn't always ugly, that he might actually been kind of cool-looking once.

"It's been a while, Latoya," he says in his weird, rumbling voice.

"Yeah," says my mom, never taking her eyes off him.

He turns to me. "Is this...? My! She's the image of you when you were young. How are you, my dear?"

"I'd appreciate if you don't address my daughter. Talk to me. Leave her out of it."

The old man shrugs and laughs, sounding like he's growling down in his throat.

Stones comes back to the table with the maître d who's holding a bottle of wine. The maître d holds the bottle in front the old man, who leans in close to the label squinting at it with his only eye. He nods. The maître d pours the wine into the old man's glass, giving the bottle a little twist. He puts the bottle on the table and disappears again.

The old guy holds the wine glass up to the light, twirling it a little.

"Hmm!" he says, watching the wine swirl around inside. He holds the glass up to his nose and sniffs it.

"Ha!" he says. Then he takes a little sip, looking up at the ceiling and blinking his eye real fast as if something got caught in it.

"Hmmmmmm. Best wine in the cellar," he says to my mom. "Join me?"

"No, thank you. I'm fine."

Mom sticks her fork into her plate, and puts some food into her mouth. Her hand is still on my thigh, and she squeezes it and nods at my plate, but I don't feel like eating anymore. I can't take my eyes off the old dude, although mom always says not to stare. He kinda creepy and kinda funny at the same time. I never had seen anyone like him before.

The maître d comes back balancing a plate on his hand and places it in front of the old guy. He picks up the napkin from the table, flicks it open, and rests it on the old man's knee. Then he turns and walks away, and Stones steps back, and stands, feet planted wide apart, behind the old man's chair.

"Thank you, Mr. Stones," says the old dude. He bows his head over his plate and starts to pray.

My mom rolls her eyes.

The old dude opens his eye and picks his fork up, holding it in a weird way, and I realize it's because he only has one arm his left arm. The other sleeve is empty and pinned to his jacket. It's obvious he ain't a born leftie. Man, someone really did a number on this guy.

"Mercedes," mom says real soft. "Aren't you going to eat your food?"

I pick up my fork and twirl it between my fingers, trying not to stare at the old man.

"Latoya," he says, chomping loud on his veggies, "you know I've always favored you."

My mom don't say anything, but she seems to prick up her ears and listen really hard.

"You've always been a darling girl," he says. "And Ronnie has always been loyal to me. Yes. My son has always been loyal."

I look up in surprise at my mom, but she shakes her head, and squeezes my thigh again.

"All my sons have not been loyal, though," says the old man, looking down at his plate. "And for years I've lived with that burden. Oh, there's nothing that breaks your heart like a disloyal son."

He hits himself over his heart with his fist. "Retribution might not always be swift, but it's always sure. This is why I want to assure you, darling girl, that your angels will be watching over you when the day of judgment comes. And your little one. I promise."

"Angels?" says my mom. She laughs like if the old dude had cracked a joke. "The only angels in my life are my husband and my baby girl."

The old dude turns his head so that his eye is looking at my mother. He smiles, making his lips go all crooked.

"If Ronald were your only angel," he says, "you would be in heaven even now. Believe that, young lady."

I stare at the old man, shocked. I look across at my mom. She's looking at her plate. Her hands are balled up into fists, like she's really upset. I thought she would scream at him or something, but she doesn't.

"What do you mean?" she questions in a quiet voice.

He shrugs and takes a sip of his wine. "You know things are not always what they seem," he says, looking sideways at me. "We can't trust everyone with a smooth face."

"I don't believe anything you say anymore," my mother spits back.

"I know that," he says, sounding sad. "But... no matter. I speak the truth."

"Truth?" my mother says with sarcasm.

"Yes, truth!" he yells all of a sudden. I drop my fork, and my mom jumps too. He looks straight at me.

"Truth isn't beautiful. It isn't pretty. Isn't dressed up in designer clothes. It's so God-awful no one wants to hear it. No one wants to get near it. My God, girl! Have you been so blinded by the comfort of your ill-gotten gains? Listen to the truth before it's too late."

My mom stares at him for a minute, as if trying to make up her mind if to take him seriously.

"I see you're still delusional, among other things," she says. "Since when do you speak the truth? Truth? Don't lay that crap on me. I know you, remember?" She tosses her napkin on the table. "Stay away from my family," she hisses at the old man. "You messed up our lives enough already."

Maurice appears by her side.

"Is everything alright, Mrs. Clinton?" he says, throwing the old man a nasty look.

"Yes, Maurice," my mom says before getting up. "We're just about to leave. Come on, Mercedes," she says to me. "Let's go, baby."

I get up, hauling our bags from under the table, glad to get away from the crazy old man.

"Leaving so soon?" says the old dude in an almost hurt tone.

Maurice and Stones eyeball each other. Stones steps aside as my mother, Maurice, and I brush past the old man.

"Even now the little birds are gathering for flight," I hear him mumble as we head for the door.

Chapter Six

Share My World

I've beat down countless men. Rode my bike through a crowd of Black Disciples shooting. Eyeballed crack dealers with semi-automatics pointed at my chest. I never felt fear. I don't know how to feel fear. Yet, the idea of proposing to Mercedes makes me so nervous, I feel I might do something stupid, like drop the ring. I feel inside my jacket and to my relief it's still there.

If looks could kill, Ronald Clinton's eyes would have cut my heart right out of my chest. I'm sure he would have fed it to the dogs. But looks can't kill, and I don't care what he thinks about me. And just to show that I'm a nice guy and don't hold no hard feelings, I go up to him and hold out my hand, as my dad had just done. I feel his body stiffen as we lean in for a blood hug.

Mercedes looks beautiful tonight. The gown with the low-plunging neckline shows off her curves and the diamonds make her look glamorous in a Hollywood Movie Star type way. I can't take my eyes off her, but I don't want to spook her out by staring at her all the time. There are mirrors on all the walls, and if I look at the one just opposite our table, I can stare at Mercedes all night without her noticing.

She takes a seat next to her mother, who suddenly looks over at me with a serious expression on her face. I smile at her, but she doesn't smile back, just stretches her lips a little. I don't stop smiling, though, cause I know that even though she don't smile much, she a real nice lady. I'm also remembering how once my dad told me he used to check for her hard and I can see why.

I sit down beside my moms, who been busy doing what she does best arranging people and things. Wait till I unleash my little surprise. She'll have so many new plans to make, she'll think she done gone to heaven. She leans over and kisses me.

My dad and Ronnie Clinton sit at opposite ends of the table. I glance at my dad. He looks over at me, locks his eyes into mine. I been feeling for a while that he wants to tell me something, but he never does. I search his eyes, trying to get a feel for what's on his mind, but he turns his head and stands up as the majordomo brings over a big bottle of bubbly.

"Family and friends," he says. "I just wanna say how glad I am to be here wit y'all tonight. Time has been good to us. Time has brought us wealth beyond our wildest dreams. It has brought us beautiful children. Time has separated us, and has brought us together again. I look forward to rekindling old friendships and enjoying good times again, and multiplying times infinity the wealth with which we've been so amazingly blessed. I also wanna take this opportunity to tell y'all that my candidacy for the race for mayor of this great city has been officially confirmed by the Board of Commissioners."

EVERYBODY CLAPS. I LOOK over at Dalvin. He's smiling a big, wide smile at his dad. Mayor! Wow! That's big.

"Thank you, thank you," says Mr. Dewitt, holding up both hands and smiling real broad as if he already won the election. "My brother, Ronnie, will be handling my public relations, media image, and that kind of thing, but more on that later. Right now, I wanna make a toast."

We stand up and lift our glasses of champagne.

"To love," says Mr. Dewitt, looking hard at his son. "To family. To life that lasts forever."

We all sip from our glasses.

Then Dalvin comes around to my side of the table. He had left his cane at home, and he walks perfectly without it. He don't limp or anything. He look strong and perfect, just like he was before he got shot.

Everybody's eyes are on him as he comes and stands in front of me. Then he goes smoothly down on one knee, pulling a little box out of his jacket. He opens it. People at the other tables look over at us.

I put my hand over my heart because for a minute it actually stops beating and I can't breathe. It's like I can't see, can't hear. The whole world seems to have faded out, and there was no one in it, but Dalvin and me.

"Mercedes," he says. His voice shakes a little. He looks up at me, his face serious.

"BABY, I LOVE YOU," I say. Her hand is resting just above her breast, and she's glowing. Her beauty is causing me to become speechless to the point I almost forget my lines. I quickly regroup.

"I loved you from the day I first laid eyes on you. You more precious to me, baby, than life itself, and I want to share my life, my world, with you for all time; take care of you, make you the happiest woman on earth. Will you marry me?"

"Yes!" she yells out. "Yes, yes." She bounces a little on her toes, like she always does when she's happy.

I stretch out my hand, and she puts hers in it. I slide the ring onto her slender finger.

I hear them clapping my mother and father, my future in-laws, the folks at the other tables as I stand up and kiss her lips... my future wife.

DALVIN HOLDS ME TIGHT as he kisses me. I hear the ooohs and aaahs from people at the other tables and the clapping and whistling. I can just imagine the look on my father's face.

He releases me, just a little, and I look into his eyes. I see so much love there, I feel the tears come streaming up from my heart and spill out of my eyes. I try to dab them away with my fingertips, but they just keep coming. All of a sudden, I feel as if I had just stepped off the edge of the world and I'm standing in mid-air. I mean, I been waiting for this moment for so long, and now that it's happening, I don't know what to do.

Then my mom is beside me. I turn to her and she hugs me. I feel her tears mingle with mine. Then Mrs. Dewitt hugs me as if she's my mother.

"You're beautiful, my darling," she whispers as she kisses me on my cheek. "Welcome to our family."

She turns to my mother, and they hug each other. My father and Dalvin's dad look pleased with themselves, as if they think the whole thing is their idea. Mr. Dewitt comes over.

"I'm proud to call you my daughter," he says, kissing me.

When my daddy kisses me, I melt. He holds me close to him real gentle, and for a moment, I wish things could go back to how they were when

I was little and I would lie against his chest for hours, tracing the pattern of the tattoo on his arm, listening to the beat of his heart, babbling on about all kind of little girl things, knowing that nothing could hurt me. The tears keep coming.

"It's okay, baby girl," he whispers. "Everything's okay. You doing just fine."

Then he releases me, and I look in his face and see how much he loves me, and I know he's right. Everything is okay.

Dalvin takes my hand again and turns to my father.

"Don't worry, Mr. Clinton," he says in a soft, serious voice. "I'll take care of her. I promise."

My dad nods, and actually smiles a grim little smile at D.

"Lemme see the ring!" squeals my mother.

The rock in my engagement ring was so massive I could almost see my face in it. My mom and Mrs. Dewitt are completely blown away as I stretch out my hand for all three of us to admire.

Chapter Seven

We Meet Again

The target, his father, and uncle tried to vanish inside the military facility. Or I should say they tried to erase their electronic footprints by doing the obvious thing discarding all their GPS-enabled devices, which made them instantly drop off everybody's radar. Then they ditched their cars and drove out in a black armored vehicle.

There was a time when eagle-eyed boun-ty-hunters on horseback stalked fugitives across miles of uneven terrain following trails of crushed leaves and broken twigs. Then came your Sherlock Holmes-type intellectual sleuth, a bit more sophis-ticated, but elementary, still, followed by the mod-ern PI.

Today, you can track a fugitive anywhere in the world using a standard laptop and cracking into the huge network of surveillance satellites conveniently created by the military which allows them access to real-time images of every human being on the planet 24/7/365. Although NASA is always denying the existence of such satellites, they're up there. Oh yeah. Big Brother is watching.

Using basic triangulation, I pick up their location after they leave the facility. Retrieving and reviewing the stored images of their journey is a long and tedious process, even with my advanced tracking software. I create a trajectory from the route they've taken over the past five months from which it's obvious that they're heading to Mexico.

I email Dalvin a map of the route, pinpointing Jacob's location right now in Texas, and a reasonable prediction of where he'll be tomorrow and the next day.

I also send him images of the military facility and its sweet little weapons cache as well as copies of all the company's files.

✵ ✵ ✵

"I KNOW THE FIRST THING I want for my trousseau," I say to my mom. We had just registered my wedding, and her, Dalvin's mom, and me are still browsing inside the shop.

"What's that?" she says, holding a crystal wine glass up to the light.

My upcoming wedding had kind of thrown my mom and Dalvin's mom together, though they didn't have an awful lot in common. Mrs. Dewitt or Mama Miriam as I call her now, since she's gonna be my mother-in-law is the daughter of a high court judge and has a business degree from Yale. My mother grew up in the projects and barely finished high school. Mama Miriam throws a dinner party every other week. My moms hardly talks to anyone besides our family down South, and she only does that on somebody's birthday. Mama Miriam has probably flown to every country on the planet in her private jet. My moms hardly goes anywhere, and it's not because she can't. She just one of those people that keep to themselves. But if there's one thing they both love to do, it's shop. Mama Miriam is an expert at that, and so is my mom. And so am I, for that matter, but they know where to get the really good stuff.

I pick up a pretty box decorated with real dried flowers. Inside is a set of love letter napkins. The letters are actual letters written by famous people printed on nice linen.

"I want something that smells sweet and sexy," I say, thinking of the last time I was with D at his condo just outside the city. He lives with his mom and dad, but he also has his own place where he kicks it back sometimes on his own.

Soft music was on, and the only light came from scented candles. The hot water in the jacuzzi felt good on my body. He slipped into the water and came close to me. I reached for the sponge, holding it under the water till it filled up, then I squeezed the water out over my head. He smiled and sucked the water off my neck and shoulders as it trickled over me. I closed my eyes, loving how his lips felt on me. He brushed his mouth over mine. I wrapped my arm around his head and pulled him to me and kissed him deep and long and hard. I ran my hands over his biceps. His hands roamed over my body.

"A fragrance?" I hear Mrs. Dewitt say.

"Not just a fragrance," I say, the scent of D lingering in my mind for a moment more before I brush it away. "More like a bath oil something you put in the tub and soak in. And lotion. Something you slather on that makes you feel soft all over. And a fragrance. And candles."

"What kind of fragrance you want?" asks Mama Miriam.

"Roses," I say. "I love roses. Think he'd like roses on me?"

"I think he'll like anything on you," says Mama Miriam, laughing.

"Really?" I say.

"Child, he so in love you could be in hair rollers with purple grease all over your face and he'll like it."

I laugh at that.

"Mercedes don't never walk around like that, though," says my mother. "That girl so vain, she put on face powder just to go downstairs to the kitchen."

"Mom!" I say embarrassed. "You don't gotta tell her that. Besides, it's only a teeny bit of face powder. Just to hide a pimple or two."

"This is gorgeous," says my mom, picking up a silver hand mirror studded with semi-precious stones. "You like this, baby?"

"It's pretty," I say, fingering the delicate design on the back. "Oh, I know what else I want for my trousseau."

"What?" she says.

"Silk sheets," I say and laugh. They laugh too.

✡ ✡ ✡

BIG CLUSTERS OF DARK clouds sit over the Chicago skyline, making it look cold and hostile. That's the mood I'm in as I look out the glass walls of my penthouse office in the building owned by my father. I scroll through the images Spider sent to my iPhone.

So Jacob, uptown Ivy League rich kid with all your fancy talk, you nothing but a thug like anybody else. So why you been fronting all this time, huh? Pretending to be somebody you ain't. And so what if you got mad back-up? I got mad back-up too, and I'll swat you like the little fly you are.

I text Spider and tell him to keep the sneaky snake in his sights, and I call my boys. I tell Demetrius to have my father's helicopter ready. I look at the time on my phone. I can get over there, pop Jacob, his father, and his uncle and be back in time to take Mercedes to lunch.

✡ ✡ ✡

"DID YOU HAVE A trousseau, Mama Miriam?"

"No, doll, I did not." She smiles warmly. "The circumstances surrounding my courtship were... touchy, to say the least. We didn't have time to think up fancy stuff like that."

Mama Miriam's father, a well-respected judge in the city, had vowed that she would never marry Dalvin's dad and had used his power and connections to destroy him. He even had him thrown in prison, but he had beat that rap. When her family turned their backs on her, she had nowhere to go. Dalvin's father supported her. He even paid her college tuition. It wasn't until her son was born that Mama Miriam became reunited with her father.

"That's such a sad story," I say, "with a happy ending. Like mine."

"I like happy endings," says my mother.

"Me too," says Mama Miriam, looking at a pair of Swarovski crystal candle holders.

"I think I want to get married in the spring."

"Mmmm," says my mom. "A spring wedding..."

She and Mama Miriam look at each other.

"Tulips..." says Mama Miriam.

"Daffodils..." says my mom.

"White roses..." says Mama Miriam.

"Ohhh," says my mom, "a yellow and white theme..."

"Doves..." Mama Miriam suggests.

"You sure you wanna do spring?" my mom asks.

"No," I say. "Yeah. I think so... Or maybe summer is better. But I like spring too."

"Yeeaaah," says my mom, looking at me doubtfully.

Mama Miriam laughs. "Oh, there's nothing more wonderful than youthful ambivalence."

"Youthful what?" I raise an eyebrow.

"Ambivalence. When you in that blissful place between options."

"Oh," I say, as she and my mom laugh.

The truth is that although I can't wait to be with Dalvin, all of a sudden I don't wanna leave my parents.

"Well," says my moms, hooking her arm into mine, "why don't we look at some spring themes as well as summer themes."

"Latoya," says Mama Miriam, "we should set a schedule. We gotta lotta things to do, whether it's summer or spring."

"Yeah," says my mom, "but we should think of a date, even a tentative one. Any thoughts on that, sweetie?"

"Ummm no," I stutter.

"Oooooh," coos Mama Miriam.

"You ain't getting cold feet are you now, baby?" sings my mom.

"No Ma," I say, feeling the tears pricking my heart again.

"Okay, baby, okay," she says, patting my arm and pecking me on the cheek. "It's gonna be alright."

Now that my wedding is becoming a reality, I can't believe how emotional I've become. I mean, I'm crying at every little thing. What's up with that?

✡ ✡ ✡

THE SOUND OF GUNSHOTS shatter my nightmare, and I struggle, half-asleep, to sit up in the bed. My father is already beside me, his Sig in one hand, his other arm draped around me, helping me up.

"That's them," he says, flashing me a fierce look.

As we move towards the door, I reach for our bags at the foot of the bed.

"Leave em," he says. "No time."

"Where's Uncle Steve?" I question.

"He went to the store. But he ain't coming back."

"Why not?"

"Cause he's dead. They got him."

"How you know that?"

"I know Dalvin."

We reach the door. He cracks it open and listens for sounds from the hallway. It's quiet. We slip outside and down the stairway to the lobby of the motel.

"Wait here," he says.

I stand by the door as he goes outside. I watch through the glass in the door as he dashes through the parking lot towards the truck and reverses it like a crazy man up to the door. I get in and he tears out of the parking lot.

The roar and thunder of the helicopter is deafening, as if it's right on top of us. I look up through the windshield. It's about fifty feet above us, swooping like a vicious bird. I hear the bullets spray the truck and the ground.

The metal bird arcs up in the air. My father steps on the gas. We're moving targets out here, without the cover of skyscrapers and tight knots of traffic.

The helicopter flies ahead of us then doubles back and comes straight at us. I see Dalvin. I know he can't see me through the tinted glass of our armored SUV, but he raises his Bushmaster and points it straight at me as if he could. The three guys with him raise their guns too. Bullets hit the truck like fire and hailstones.

"Get down, Jacob!" my dad hollers as he makes a crazy u-turn that sends the truck flipping over.

I hear the bullets like thunder spray down on us. The truck flips twice, and then I black out.

✡ ✡ ✡

I CALL AGAIN, AGAIN and it goes to voicemail. I take a sip of water, tap my nails on the table and look around. It's the same restaurant I was at with my moms a couple days ago. She and Mama Miriam had dropped me there and gone off together with the shopping bags in the limo, talking 'bout wedding dates and wedding themes. I check the time. I'm impatient. Not just because I'm dying to see him, but I really hate waiting and I'm hungry. But I want to wait for my fiancé and eat with him. I love that word now... fiancé. I smile to myself. Then I see him strolling through the restaurant towards me. He leans over and kisses me before sitting down.

"Sorry I'm late, Mercy," he says. "I had some business to take care of out of town. Been waiting long?"

"Oh, that's okay, D," I say. "I ain't been waiting long. Only about 10 minutes. I ordered for both of us."

"Cool," he says. He smiles at me, but his eyes are distant. He takes out his phone and scrolls through it. He's silent. Withdrawn.

"Everything alright, babe?" I ask.

"Yeah," he says, looking up at me for a moment.

His eyes are so hard my heart skips a beat. He rests his hand gently on mine. "What'd you order?"

"Smoked salmon for you, salad for me."

"Sounds good," he says, sliding the phone into his pocket. A waiter brings our plates, and the maître d walks up to our table. I remember him from the last time I was in here with my mother. He was the one who had brought the old dude his wine.

"Is everything to your liking, sir?" he says to D.

"Yeah," D shakes his head, almost as if he didn't hear him. "Everything's cool." He pulls out his phone again.

The maître d walks on by. I watch as he walks through the restaurant and stops at another table. I blink in amazement when I see who's over there.

"I can't believe it," unable to contain how astounded I am.

"What?" D wants to know.

"That old dude," I inform him. "He in here again."

"What old dude?"

"Behind us."

D shifts his gaze to look behind me.

"Don't look," I say. "He might come over here."

"Who's he?" he says, glancing at his phone.

"You know, I don't know. He never said his name, but my mom knows him. He's a creepy old guy, though. Old and skinny with a black patch over his eye."

Dalvin looks up suddenly.

I SEEN THAT OLD dude before, but I don't remember where. I heard his name too, but I can't remember what it is. I hold the image of the old man in my mind, trying to place him, but the effort frustrates me, like I'm tryna remember the details of a dream. I push away thoughts about him and try to focus on Mercedes. I look into her pretty almond-shaped eyes and smile. I see the truck flipping over as I fire my Bushmaster.

Spider had directed me straight to the motel where Jacob and his father were hiding. I watch as his father ran into their truck like a little cockroach. I was so tickled I laughed out loud. You can run, Adam Powers, but you can't hide.

We follow them at an easy pace and float down slowly till we're almost sitting on their truck, then me and my boys rain down fire on them. I hear Spider in my earbuds telling me a police patrol helicopter is in the area. We bank and fly out of there with plenty time to spare.

But I'm pissed. Spider just sent me a text saying Jacob and his father were airlifted out of the car wreck and taken to the hospital. They're both still alive.

I HEAR THE WHIRRING noise behind me, and know that the old man is approaching. I bend my head over my plate as he drives straight by us with Stones beside him, heading for the door.

D glances up from his phone as they pass, just as Stones looks over at our table. D wasn't paying them much mind. He was more interested in his phone. But Stones stares at him as he swaggers, hands in his pockets, towards the door. It's such a direct, deliberate, amused look, it holds D's attention, and he kind of snaps his head back as if he thought someone had smacked him in the face. He stares at Stones, looking surprised, then pissed.

"Yo," says D as Stones continues to eye him, "what's your problem, son?"

Stones don't say nothing, just looks at D and I get the feeling he knows him.

"What you looking at?" says D in a loud voice. People look around at us, and the maître d comes hurrying up to our table.

"Is there a problem sir?" he says to D.

"This punk keeps staring at me, yo," says D, getting up from the table, but Stones and the old dude are already out the door.

"I'm so sorry that you are disturbed, sir," says the maître d. "It won't happen again."

D stares at them through the glass wall as they wind their way through the people outside.

"Do you know him, D?" I ask.

"No," he says. "Do you?"

"No. But he seems to know you. And the old man knows my mom."

"Really?" says D, his hard eyes fixed on Stones and the old dude as they get into a limo that pulls up to the curb.

✡ ✡ ✡

HIS FACE IS LIKE a shadow in the gloom. He sits beside me, looking at me out of one eye, and I wonder if I'm dreaming again. I want to ask him about my dad, if he's alright, but my lids are so heavy I can't keep them open. Darkness closes in on me.

When I open my eyes again, he's gone. The sensation I felt of pain and nausea as our truck rolls over floods through me again suddenly. I close my eyes. The beeping sound of the machine gets fainter until it fades to nothing.

✡ ✡ ✡

THE ROOM IS DARK, but the images Spider feeds into my phone are clear. I see Jacob hooked up to several machines by IV tubes, just like I was months ago. I savor how it feels to see the scum getting a taste of his own medicine. He tried to kill me, and he almost did, and I won't rest till he gets his. Ain't karma a big ole nasty mofo?

I scroll till I can see the side of the room. There are two police officers guarding the door. I laugh out loud. Oh no, Jacob. Cops ain't gonna save you.

"Spider," I say into my phone. "Are there cops outside his door?"

"Yeah," he comes back.

"How many guarding the father?"

"Same," he says. "Two inside and two outside."

A dark shadow cuts across the camera in the room, and I'm suddenly disturbed, not knowing what to make of this persistent presence.

"Spider," I say. "See that old dude in the wheel-chair next to Jacob's bed?"

I don't hear him, and I wonder if his phone went dead.

"Spider," I say.

"He's in my sights," says Spider.

"I wanna know his name," I say. "I wanna know everything about him."

Chapter Eight

I Am My Father's Daughter

"These are just conceptual sketches," says Melinda in her New York accent. "We can mix and match and you can change the color scheme however you want." She's a recent Pratt Institute grad doing an internship at Sophie's, one of the top bridal boutiques in the state. She looks kind of nervous as she spreads the sketches out on the table in Dalvin's kitchen. My mom smiles at her.

"Nice," says Mama Miriam, leaning over the table to get a closer look at one of the sketches. Selena hovers behind us with a tray of steaming mugs.

"Just put them here, Selena," sings Mama Miriam, moving aside one of the sketches in the center of the table and easing into the chair beside me.

Selena places the mugs on the table and backs away, returning after a moment with another tray piled with scones, muffins, and brownies. I take one of the sweet-smelling cups and blow into it. The TV is on, and Dalvin's dad, looking fly and cool like the president, is on Talk to the Press.

"Oh, I like this," says my mom, pointing to one of the sketches and taking a sip of her mocha. Her eyeglasses are sitting at the end of her nose, and as she pulls her cardigan closer around her, she looks so pretty and cozy and homey, I feel I wanna snuggle up to her and never let her go. I swallow down tears and hot chocolate.

"What do you think, sugarplum?" she says, tracing one of the sketches with her finger.

I don't know what I think. I shift my eyes to the TV.

"Mr. Dewitt," the interviewer is saying, "Chicago has one of the highest homicide rates in the country. How do you intend to tackle this problem if you were to become mayor of this city?"

"Well, Douglas," Mr. Dewitt places the tips of his fingers together. "I think we need to take a two-fold approach to this. The first approach is, of course, stiffer gun control legislation..."

"Gun control?" Douglas cuts in. "Do you think Americans will go for that?"

"You know, we have to face reality," says Mr. Dewitt. "We do have a problem here, and there does have to be some measure of control. But we need to take a multi-level approach. The other approach is to tackle the problem of violence at the level of the community..."

"...you're talking about community-based programs..."

"Yes, like education programs, arts programs, creative programs that help young people deal with issues of self-esteem..."

✡ ✡ ✡

THE RECEPTIONIST IS PRETTY. She looks up and smiles at me as I approach the desk.

"Good afternoon, sir," she says. "How may I help you?"

"I'm looking for my cousin," I say, giving her my Doublemint smile. "His name is Jacob. Jacob Powers."

She quickly searches through the hospital database.

"Oh, yes, sir. He's in Room 301. Just go along the hallway and take a right then a left. His is the second door."

"Thank you, miss," I say as I swing down the hall. I didn't expect any problems. I had called in a couple favors the police chief owed me. Sure enough, there were no policemen at his door.

I went in, closing the door behind me, and stood just inside the room while my eyes adjusted to the dim light. I slide my hand inside my jacket as I approach his bed and grip the butt of my Glock with the silencer attached. But Jacob isn't in the bed. I swing round, my eyes scanning the room. It's empty. I pull out my weapon holding it close to my chest as I walk slowly through the room.

"May I help you sir?"

I slide my gun back into the holster under my jacket and turn around. A nurse is standing at the door.

"Hi," I say, giving him my best confused smile. "I came to see my cousin, but it seems he's not here."

"Oh, Mr. Powers has been discharged," he says.

"Discharged? By whom?"

"He and his father checked themselves out. They left only a few minutes ago. If you hurry, you might catch them before they leave."

"Thanks," I say, brushing past him out the door. I walk quickly down the hallway, my eyes searching the faces of everyone I pass. I reach the exit and stand outside scanning the sidewalk.

Adam and Jacob Powers had disappeared without a trace. Again.

✧ ✧ ✧

"AND A CORNERSTONE OF your campaign is tackling gang violence..."

"Yes," says Mr. Dewitt smiling into the camera, "I intend to approach this problem head-on, and bring down the homicide rate by ten percent in the first year of my tenure as mayor..."

"Oooh," sings my mom, "look at the little swans..."

"Yes," says Melinda, "this is the Swan Lake theme. I love this one. Isn't it romantic?"

"It sure is," coos my mom.

"I love the swan ice sculptures," says Mama Miriam, nibbling on a scone. "What do you think, doll?"

"They're nice," I say.

"Do you like the yellow and white color scheme?" Melinda asks me, "or do you prefer the blue and white?"

"Ummm yeah," I say, "but I like the multi-colored one better. It's prettier."

"It sure is," says my moms.

My mind wanders from the conversation at the kitchen table.

"...do you stand in the gun control debate? Conservative? Liberal?"

I prick up my ears to hear what Mr. Dewitt's gonna say about that, cause I'm carrying a gun in my purse.

The day after the dinner party, the day after the old man with the patch approached us in the restaurant, mom and dad and me were having dinner at home in the kitchen. Everybody's really quiet. My father seems to be thinking about something deep, and from time to time he would look up at me like he was sizing me up or something. My mom's mind seemed to be far away. My mind was all over the place. I'm thinking about what D said to me when he put the ring on my finger. I'm thinking about Stones, the way he looked at me, as if he was seeing into my soul, or something. I'm thinking about the old man and the things he said to my mom. I couldn't figure out what he meant. I wanted to ask my dad, but I knew he'd be mad. When my mom got up to clear away the plates, he got up too and went into his study.

"'Night, mom," I said, going to the sink and giving her a kiss.

"Good night, Sugarplum," she said, kissing me back, her big, brown eyes seeming to want to tell me something.

"What's wrong?" I asked her.

"Nothing, baby," she said, bending her head over the plates in the sink.

Yeah, yeah. Same ole, same ole. Nobody ever tells me anything. I made up my mind I'm not going to ask my dad nothing, cause he ain't gonna give me a straight answer. I'll ask D. He's the only one who ever tells me the truth. And he'll know. He has a way of getting answers to anything.

I went up to my room and laid on my bed. I stretched out my hand, admiring my engagement ring, feeling excited; my love for D warming me like a soft, winter blanket. I think about the home we'll make together, all the fun we'll have decorating, and our babies. I wanna have, like, five babies. They're gonna look a little bit like D and a little bit like me. They gonna be so cute. Then the old man's face flashed into my thoughts, and a dark cloud seemed to overshadow everything. He called my father his son. What did he mean by that? And why can't I get him out of my head?

"Princess? It's Daddy," he said, knocking at my door. He opened it and walked into my room. He hesitated before coming over to my bed and sitting down. He sighed a heavy sigh and pulled something out of his pocket. I look at the little gun, sitting snug in the palm of his hand, not knowing what to think.

For most of my life, I had lived in ignorance of the things going on around me. My family is mega-rich, and I just took it all for granted. My life was like one nonstop party of fun. I completely over-indulged in everything I wanted which mostly included shopping and hanging out. Then I met D. He was the one who told me my father was the head of a crime family. That jolted me out of my haze, alright, but not as much as it should have.

Even when D got shot I still didn't get it. I mean, that should have opened my eyes, right? But it didn't. I knew Jacob was the one who shot him, and at first, I thought it was because D beat him down the night he tried to rape me in his car. But then, I began to hear things—little pieces of things I didn't understand. Or was it that the pieces of things I had been hearing all my life seemed suddenly to have deeper meanings from before? I now knew I had been missing important pieces of a big, complicated puzzle, and I didn't know what they were. I didn't even know how to begin to find out.

I snap out of my thoughts and back at Mr. Dewitt on the TV screen, smiling that cool smile of his.

"I'm very conservative on the issue of protecting lives," he says, "but I believe there are certain liberties that are sacrosanct, including the liberty to protect yourself, so that gun control needs to be approached intelligently and strategically..."

I hear my mother call my name and I try to force my mind to think about the sketches in front of me.

"We want to make an appointment for a fitting," my mom says to me. "We can get Wednesday the twenty-seventh or Thursday the twenty-eighth. Which one do you want, baby?"

She gets up from the table and fishes in the big wicker basket we had brought with us from the house. She gently lifts out her wedding dress and shakes it out of the tissue paper. Melinda is blown away.

"Oooh," she says, fingering the stones. "This is hands down the most gorgeous wedding dress I've ever seen. Who's the designer?"

"Me and my grandma," says my mom, and she and Mama Miriam laugh as Melinda's jaw drops open, like mine did when my dad gave me the gun. I looked into his eyes, thinking he might be playing with me, but he was dead serious.

"It's a Smith and Wesson," he says, his voice low and serious. "I'm gonna show you how to break it down, I'm gonna show you how to clean it and how to reassemble it. And tomorrow, I'm gonna take you to the range and show you how to shoot it."

"Daddy?" I sat up in my bed. The old dude had flashed through my mind again, his face like a death head. I'm suddenly scared.

"I know," he said. "Don't be scared, baby. I didn't want it to come to this, but you might need it one day. It's not enough to just keep you away from trouble, cause sometimes trouble just come right up in your face, and next time it does, I want you to know what to do."

I looked at the gun my overprotective father had given me, and wondered for a wild moment if he knew.

"Dad," I said, "the other day when me and mom were having lunch, an old man came to our table."

He looked at me. His face is hard, and suddenly, I'm sure he knows.

"Who is he, Daddy?" I ask. "Who's that old man?"

Chapter Nine

The Oath

I was five years old when my father was murdered, and I've been living in his ever-present shadow ever since. My mom kept him alive from the day The Shepherd came to our house to tell us he had been tortured to death. Our house became a kind of shrine to him and all he did. Richard Stones. Wealthy and successful entrepreneur. Community leader. Defender of the people. Cut down in his prime by the Mafia. He was my very own, larger than life hero whose impossibly large shoes I was asked to fill.

When I was a kid, I kept a photograph of him next to my bed, and every night I'd gaze at it, trying to conjure into flesh and blood the spirit of the image I saw there, thinking maybe I carried some of his greatness inside me.

He was tall and fit, with a well-defined, muscular body, like the other men in the photo—Ronnie Clinton and Dalvin Dewitt on one side, Isaiah Jones and Adam Powers on the other—their arms carved with tattoos of the snake eating its tail, the symbol of infinity, the symbol Shepherd adopted as the insignia of the Brotherhood. You can actually feel their intensity, which isn't surprising, given the crazy things The Shepherd put them through. He was in the picture too, next to Dalvin, tall and strong and able-bodied like his sons, both eyes looking directly into the camera.

I look into my father's eyes. They're cool, intelligent eyes. Unyielding. Fearless. The eyes of the father I missed so much.

With my dad gone, Shepherd became a kind of evil stepfather to me. Even though I was just a little kid, my mom delivered me completely into his hands. He dreamed his nightmares into me, fed me his megalomaniacal fantasies, scooped out my soul and filled me with himself, lived his life again through me.

Do I regret those early years when I feared him so much I tried with everything in me to be what he wanted me to be even though all my instincts told me different? A little, but not enough to moan about. For every bit of the childhood innocence he stole from me, I gained so much more in knowledge and personal power.

I was kept apart from other kids who didn't

have a hero's legacy hanging over them and a guardian who watched their every move. The only kid who felt me was Jimmy Jones, whose father, Isaiah, was shot in the head by the traitor and left to die in an alley. At least, that's the way Shepherd always tells it.

Jimmy was my only friend. He was so small and skinny and nerdy we called him Incy Wincy Spider, or Spider for short. He wasn't much of a fighter, and so all through grade school, I had to keep him under my wing, just to keep him from getting beat up every day, cause what he lacked in size and muscle, he more than made up for with his smart-ass mouth. You know how many kids I had to pop because of him? Shepherd fussed over him, called him his prize, even talked of sending him to a special school for the gifted, but his mother put her foot down at that cause Spider didn't want to go. I don't think Shepherd ever forgave her.

Then when he was 13, his amazing computer skills earned him his first arrest for cracking into the computer network of a bank and shutting it down using one of his own original viruses. He didn't do time, though, cause it was a first offense and he didn't actually steal anything. He got off with a slap on the wrist. After that, he didn't need my protection anymore. He kind of just came into his own.

We stuck together throughout high school, and then went off to college, but Spider, who felt he was smarter than his professors—and I think he actually was—dropped out and retreated into cyberspace, where he crawls around like a real arachnid in the never-ending world wide web.

Shepherd insisted that I go to Princeton. I graduated with a law degree and went to work for him.

It was Spider who figured out how to break the circle. After all, cracking codes is his specialty, and not just computer codes either. Evidently, he's just as good at cracking dream codes. That was when we dropped that subtle hint to Dalvin's side-kick, Demetrius. Spider has a way of reaching out to people that makes them think they've reached out to him. They did exactly what we expected, and Spider and Dalvin have been in constant communication since then, collaborating on Dalvin's obsession—finding Jacob.

But me and Spider have our own reasons for wanting to locate Jacob after he went MIA. We need him. We need Dalvin too, and Mercedes, though I foresee that Dalvin's over-the-top tendency to put the fear of God into people could become a serious problem.

It's Shepherd's desire that the offspring of the original Brotherhood come together again to form a new, more dangerous star. But as long as I'm alive, that ain't gonna happen. Oh, there's gonna be a new star alright, but not the one The Shepherd's thinking about.

"DID YOU FOLLOW UP your meeting with the Senator, Mr. Stones?" he asks as we maneuver through a knot of people on the sidewalk. I scan the street for the limo.

"Yes, I did, Shepherd," I answer him. "I called him this morning."

"And what did he say?"

"They're going to propose a committee to discuss opening an investigation."

"Propose a committee?" He's amused. "...to discuss...? I want you to keep on that, Mr. Stones. I want him completely exposed before he meets his maker. Discredited. Broken. Ruined. For everyone to see."

"Here's the limo," I say, as our ride rounds the corner.

"Beautiful day."

I turn. He's standing right up under my elbow. I almost laugh out loud. We were expecting him, and knew he would show up in his own time in his own way.

"Ronnie!" Shepherd sounds glad to see him, but Ronald Clinton had been Shepherd's first protégé, or disciple, or victim, depending on your point of view. He knew who he was dealing with.

"Hello, Shepherd," he says. He sounds cool, but his face is hard.

"It's such a pity you didn't join us earlier," says Shepherd as the limo pulls up to the curb. "We would have loved to have you lunch with us."

"That's okay," says Ronnie. He looks at me, his eyes seeming to search for a sign of recognition of his murdered blood brother.

The door to the limo is open and the ramp descends gently onto the sidewalk.

"Please," says Shepherd, driving his wheelchair into the limo, "get in, get in."

I enter and sit beside Shepherd. Ronnie Clinton eases into the seat opposite us.

He's in his forties, maybe the age my father would have been had he lived. There's a certain stamp Shepherd leaves on the men he influences. They all carry themselves with a swagger, a sense of entitlement, a subtle threat of violence. Ronnie's demeanor suggests that he's used to getting his way.

"Here's the thing, Shepherd," he says as the limo drives off. "I don't want you near my family. If you come near my wife and daughter again I'll kill you."

Shepherd laughs a deep, rumbling belly laugh of pure enjoyment.

"Ronnie," he says, "never one to mince words. I was delighted to converse with your charming wife after all these years. Laytoya looks very well, and your little one..."

Ronnie leans forward till he's right up in the old man's face.

"Do I need to repeat myself, Shepherd?" he

says. "I know you getting on in years. Maybe you don't hear too good."

"I hear you, Ronnie," says Shepherd. "I hear you. But there's no need for threats. I'm not the one you should be taking out your aggression on, anyway. I thought I taught you better than that—how to identify your real enemies."

"I ain't here to get into any ideological discussion with you," Ronnie says. "Believe me when I say that I will do whatever I have to do to keep you away from my family."

"Will you?" Shepherd is suddenly very serious. "And yet you sell your only daughter to the son of a butcher, who happens to be worse than his father, in case you haven't noticed. A thug is what young Dalvin is. And a murderer. And for what? The proverbial 30 pieces of silver? I thought she was worth much more to you than just... money."

Ronnie keeps his cool. He looks out the window as we stop at a light.

"Besides," continues Shepherd, "what have I ever done to you but give you the desires of your heart?"

Ronnie turns to him, studies him.

"You wanted the girl of your dreams. I gave her to you. You wanted to be fabulously wealthy. I gave you more wealth than you imagined you could have. You wanted respect. You have it, though if it were commonly known how you acquired even a fraction of your fortune, you'd probably be subjected to the modern equivalent of a lynching."

"You think you're responsible for my success?" asks Ronnie.

"Now, now," says Shepherd, "don't go getting all ungrateful on me. You know you couldn't have done it without me. You didn't know the first thing to do to get out of the grave of your ghetto birth."

Ronnie looks hard at him, a trace of amusement in his eyes.

"I gave you life, Ronnie," says Shepherd. "And I can take it away. Believe me, son."

"You threatening me, old man?"

"Oh, I don't need to threaten you, Ronnie," Shepherd's voice is hard. "It is what it is. And it has been that way from the day you swore your first oath to me. You think that oath was a few impressive-sounding words? A nice little ritual? That oath was real. It binds you to me, body and soul, for eternity."

Ronnie Clinton glances at me. I see the question in his eyes. I look straight back at him.

"There's an infinite number of ways to die," says Shepherd. "Choose one, because death is the only way out. At least in this life."

"Your father was a good man," says Ronnie Clinton to me. "He was a good soldier, and I know he was a good father to you. He loved you very much."

I smile an obligatory smile, though the high compliment deserves much more.

"Thank you, sir," I say. The old man's chair rocks slightly as the limo turns a corner.

"I deeply regret that you didn't possess the wisdom to preserve your family from the destruction that will surely overcome them now that you're physically joining them to the family of a traitor under sentence of death. I had hoped for more from you. I'm beginning to think that my belief in you has been misplaced," Shepard says with dread in his voice.

Ronnie Clinton's eyes are still locked into mine, probing me, searching for Richard Stones. Then he shifts his eyes to The Shepherd.

"You'll never stop, will you?" he says. "They were right about you. You are the Devil."

"And you'll never wise up," growls Shepherd. "I always knew that your support of Dalvin Dewitt was because of some spell he'd cast over you, with his smooth face and his smooth talk. But I believed that in time you'd see the truth of who he was."

"I always knew who I was dealing with," says Ronnie. "He's my brother. Of course I know who he is."

"Because of him, this young man is fatherless today..."

"That's what you say..."

"That's what I know. And because of him, I'm crippled for life." He stretches out his arm. "Look what he did to me. Look!"

The pain and rage in his voice hangs in the

silence that fills the car. Ronnie looks at him, un-moved.

"Dalvin Dewitt sold you all out to the Mafia," says Shepherd in a calmer voice. "He went to the Boss and told him you were coming. There should have been no deaths. And why did he do it? Be-cause of greed. Greed. Pure and simple. He trad-ed your lives for money. The Brotherhood meant nothing to him. The very idea of brotherhood was lost on him. He sold you out then, and he'll do it again. My sentence is still in force. He may have es-caped death all those years ago, but he won't es-cape it again."

"Why continue to fight a war you can't win?" says Ronnie.

"Can't win?" Shepherd sounds genuinely sur-prised. "Whaddaya mean, Ronnie? Of course I'll win my war."

"Let it go. It's over."

"That sign you carry on your person. It means infinity. It's never over." He laughs. He sounds truly delighted. "It is never over. Why do I get the feeling you don't quite understand what that means? But you will, son Ronnie. You will."

"So here's what I want you to understand, Shepherd," says Ronnie, as the limo stops at a light. "As far as I'm concerned, the past is gone. My con-cern is with the present and the future. Don't give me a reason to kill you because if I have to, I will. I promise." He opens the door and slips outside, pulling up the collar of his coat, weaving through the cars and disappearing among the crowd in the street.

Shepherd doesn't say anything else, just sits in his chair and laughs and chuckles and giggles, clearly enjoying his private joke.

I settle back in the seat, contemplating Ronnie's Clinton's words and the way he looked at me, as if he'd read me perfectly, and understood that whatever there was of Richard Stones in me was there no longer.

Chapter Ten

No Longer A Stranger

She walks like a kitten. Her thighs are lean, butt curvaceous, abs flat, breasts round. Her skin is golden brown, smooth and clear. She wears designer clothes and an attitude that tells guys they better up their game or they'd find themselves in a crumpled heap on the curb nursing a battered ego. She had just come out of a deli, and was nibbling on an ice cream cone. I shadow her at a discreet distance, making sure her father's soldiers don't make me.

Although petite, she swings down the street with a strut like a supermodel on her own private runway, a rich girl in expensive clothes eating ice cream, ignoring the stares of the men who pass her. She puts her phone to her ear; laughs a little. Then she stops and looks around. I turn away, pretending to look at something in a shop window.

I see Dalvin reflected in the glass as he approaches her. He has the urban Wall Street look women go after, but I can clearly see the thug he really is. In the arrogant tilt of the head. In the barely subdued aggression just under the surface of the smooth exterior. He's a couple years younger than me. Not even in his twenties, but carrying himself like someone who thinks he has the world in the palm of his hand. I push away the edge of irritation I feel suddenly, reminding myself that he ain't no threat to me, because his future is in the palm of my hands.

He walks up to her and says something. She smiles, stepping close to him. He kisses her on the lips, a slow and intimate kiss, right there in the middle of the street. Then they walk hand in hand down the sidewalk, two love birds oblivious to everything and everyone around them. I watch them until a swarm of people swallows them up.

If anyone were to ask me why I've been shadowing Mercedes Clinton since that day The Shepherd barged in on her lunch with her mother, I would say that when it comes to my work I'm dedicated. But the truth is that I'm fascinated by her. I had been thinking about her all the time since that day at the restaurant. Maybe because she was strikingly beautiful. Maybe because she had this haughty way about her. Maybe because she belonged to another man and I enjoy a challenge.

✡ ✡ ✡

I DON'T KNOW HOW long he was walking beside me.
On a day I was actually able to get rid of my father's
hired soldiers, I might need them the most.

"Hello, Miss Clinton," he says. I look around,
surprised. His hands are in his pockets and he's
wearing a pair of dark glasses. He's tall like D, toned
and muscular, and his skin is dark, very fine and
smooth. He has thick black curls that fall in masses
around his head to his shoulders. He look so good,
I catch my breath. I look away before he can see the
effect he's having on me.

"What do you want?" I ask him, speeding up
my stride. He keeps pace with me.

"I don't want anything," he says in his high-
class accent. "I just happened to see you strolling
by, and I remembered you from the other day at
the restaurant, and I thought I'd say hello."

"Hello. And goodbye."

He laughs. It's a nice, musical laugh that makes
me smile, even though I try not to.

"Goodbye?" he says. "C'mon. We just met."

"Just met and just parting ways."

"Just like that?" he says. "At least lemme buy
you a cup of coffee."

I look at him. He so fine plus my curiosity
about the old man hasn't left my mind, so I can't

say no.

We swing into a Starbucks close by.

I ENJOY LOOKING AT her as she slides into the seat at the table I chose. She eases a slender thigh over her leg as she slips off her coat and sips her iced coffee. She has amazing almond-shaped eyes and full, pouty lips just waiting to be kissed.

"So what's your name again?" she says.

"Raven."

"Raven? What kinda name is that?"

"I'm part Blackfoot," I say. "That's what my name means in English. Raven Stones. You can call me Rave."

"Okay, Raven Stones. Rave," she says. "Just so you know, I'm engaged to be married, and my fiancé is mad jealous and crazy. So if you don't stop sneaking up on me like that, you might wake up and find yourself dead."

"Wake up and find myself dead? Why would I do a thing like that, pretty lady?" I say, enjoying her spirit.

"I told you. My man is crazy jealous." Although she's giving me the brush off, I can see by the look in her eyes that she's feeling me, even though she ain't smiling.

"If I was your man, I'd be crazy jealous too," I say. She's holding her cup with the hand sporting her engagement ring, and I do feel a sudden sharp sting of jealousy. "Nice rock," I must admit.

"Thanks," she says, not breaking eye contact with me as she raises the cup to her lips.

"When's the wedding?" I ask.

"Spring."

"So soon?"

"Yeah."

"You known him for a long time, then."

"Not quite a year," she divulges.

"Y'all move quick."

"Not really," she says, "considering that we had a lot of obstacles to overcome."

"Oh yeah? Like what?"

"Like my father, who didn't want us to get together."

"Why?" I ask, though I knew the answer. I had met Ronnie Clinton, and I know Dalvin Dewitt. I have a good idea what her father's beef is.

"He didn't think D was good enough for me."

He's not, but I keep my opinion to myself. "I guess he don't think anybody's good enough for his little girl, huh?"

"He's like that."

"But," I say, "love will find a way, right?"

"Right," she says.

"Mercedes, may I call you that?"

"Sure," she says. Her phone rings, and she glances at it. "Gimmie a minute... Hi baby... yeah, I'm on my way right now... just stopped at Starbucks to get a cup of coffee... yeah... I'll be right there... love you too."

She rises from the table gathering up her coat. I get up too, disappointed that our conversation is cut short.

"Gotta go," she says. "Nice talking to you, Rave."

"It was very nice talking to you too, Mercedes," I say. "Can I call you sometime?" I search her eyes for the answer behind the answer I know she'll give me.

"Of course not," she says. "I'm getting married in a few weeks."

"Well then," I say, deciding to take the plunge. "You call me." I flip out my card and hold it out to her. She takes it between the tips of her fingers and looks at it.

"Hmmmm," she says as if she had tasted something sweet, though her voice is laced with sarcasm. "Attorney-at-law."

"Call me whenever you need someone. Okay?"

She looks at me, cocking her head, confusion spreading over her face.

"When you need someone to talk to, when you need someone... to help you." She laughs at that, but I push ahead. "When you feel you need to get out of the tight little box you're in."

"What makes you think I'm in a tight little box?" she asks.

"I know you are," I say, hoping she doesn't hear the anger I suddenly felt. "The life you're born into puts you there. But if you feel the box is closing in on you, or if you have any... strange dreams... call me."

She seems to freeze for a moment, her eyes fixed on me.

"Dreams?" she says.

"Yeah."

She looks at me with bewilderment, and I feel she's about to say something. Instead, she shrugs.

"Bye, Raven."

"Bye, my beautiful Mercedes."

I watch as she winds her way through a tight knot of people. I smile at the look she'd flashed me through those big, brown eyes of hers as she turned away.

Chapter Eleven

The Wedding

"The oath was short and simple. No hard words to pronounce. Nothing complicated to do. No pain. Okay, maybe a little pain, because it was a blood oath, and my sons had to allow a small bit of their blood to be drawn. But that was all. Nothing weird like the Illuminati, or creepy like the Black Disciples. Essentially, it was an oath that bound them together, so that they shared each others' fates, and bound them to me, The Shepard, putting them under my protection as their father for eternity.

I know they didn't understand the depth of the words they swore to each other and to me. They were more interested in the wealth I promised, which, by the way, was delivered unto them all in full measure.

So Dalvin Dewitt didn't understand that his betrayal of his brothers to the Mafia was an unforgivable crime that he would pay for eternally. It's no accident that his son was almost murdered by Jacob Powers, whose father carried out the sentence of death I pronounced on him. It's also no accident he didn't die when Adam shot him, a slight oversight on my part. I'd forgotten how much it takes to kill a son of mine. I should have mentioned that to Adam. My bad. It's not accidental that both he and his son live out their days in constant pain and have both become pain med junkies. Nor is it an accident that young Dalvin and Ronnie's daughter are about to participate in another ancient ceremony that binds souls together throughout eternity, which makes them an extremely powerful force, if they only knew.

And it's not coincidental that they and the other children of my sons will be locked in a never-ending cycle of conflict and shifting allegiances for as long as the circle remains unbroken."

✡ ✡ ✡

I SLIDE MY AK INTO the scabbard on the kitchen counter, pull my sweater over my bulletproof vest and swing the scabbard over it, strapping it on snug.

I move quickly toward the door, pulling on my

leather jacket. I run down the steps to the garage, press the button to the garage door, slip on my gloves, and hop on my bike. Before the door is fully open, I'm outside with my helmet on revving my bike out of the driveway. I swing on up the street and onto the highway.

This is the moment I've been groomed for my whole life. All those long, painful years with Shepherd, all the training and self-discipline and mental programming and monkish devotion to the laws of The Brotherhood—all of it has been for the sole purpose of killing Dalvin Dewitt.

✪ ✪ ✪

I'VE BEEN LOOKING FORWARD to my wedding day since I was a little girl. I think every girl does, because it's the most special day of your life. It's the day you join yourself to the man of your dreams believing that all your romantic fantasies will finally become real and you'll live happily ever after.

My father pulled out all the stops, I mean really laid on the works at All Saints Chapel for the ceremony; at Casa Tranquilo, one of our villas ten minutes away for the reception, and everywhere in between. He put on our version of a royal wedding.

All Saints Chapel looks like a magic garden with pink and white roses streaming along its high arches, clustered along each pew and bunched together in elaborate arrangements all over the altar. The chapel smells sweet from their scent, and little bees and butterflies fly in and out attracted by the fragrance.

My wedding party has completely taken over every classroom, conference room and office in the church. The Chicago Mass Choir has two rooms. Another room is reserved for an R&B Superstar that my father paid handsomely to get. But he wanted this day to be perfect for me and locking down this crooner with the silky voice was the icing on the cake. No one will know who that is until the ceremony itself, because it's a surprise. Another room was made into a photo studio. Nicholas, my favorite celebrity stylist, turned another room into a salon, and his team of stylists and make-up artists set up little booths to do everybody's hair and make-up. Nicholas personally did mine.

"Don't you worry about nothing, honey child," he says, teasing my hair with the pointy stem of a comb. "You gonna look so ravishing that cute man of yours won't know what to do with himself."

I'm sitting on a chair in my lacy bustier, long slip, sheer silk stockings and my furry slippers. Sherry dips her make-up brush into the face power and dabs my face. All day, I've been walking around in a daze, too nervous and emotional to speak much. I just let everyone pull me here and there and do whatever they wanted to do to me.

"Look at me, darling," says Bobby, one of the

photographers hired by my father who's been taking behind the scenes shots of everybody. Nicholas places his fingertips delicately on my temples and turns my head so she could see my face. He strikes a pose, his hands poised over my head, a big, made-for-the-camera grin on his face.

"That's it. That's good," says Bobby snapping the picture.

"Oh, call me gorgeous," sings Nicholas, taking a step back and spreading his arms. "That's what's up." He comes to stand in front of me to admire his work. Bobby circles us, her Nikon to her face, snapping shot after shot.

"Baby?" my mother bustles into the room, looking amazing in a white sequined skirt suit and silver high heels. She comes over to me and takes my face in her hands, kissing me on the cheek and rubbing away the lipstick smudge with her thumb. Her perfume tickles my nose a bit.

"Now for the magic moment," says Nicholas, stretching out his hand. I put mine in it and rise from the chair. He takes me over to the rack where my gown is hung up. He and my mother unhook the dress from the hanger as if it were made of precious gold. Mom pulls down the zipper. I step into it as my mother pulls up the zipper. She smooths its lace and glamour onto my body, and I feel like I've been transformed from everyday Mercedes Clinton to some special creature. The gown seems to shimmer even more in the Hollywood lighting of the room. My mom fusses over me, Nicholas arranges the long train behind me, Sherry puts the finishing touches on my face and Bobby snaps away with her camera.

"Smile for me, mom," says Bobby.

My mother twists a little as she smooths down the gown with her hands and gives Bobby a smile.

"Oooh, that's good, Mommy." Winks Bobby.

"Oh, this train is mega-fab," says Nicholas. "Look at all these gorgeous stones in it. And it's mad long. How long is it?"

"It's ten feet long," says my mother.

"Ten feet?" gushes Nicholas, "Really? I think it's even longer than Kate Middleton's."

"It is," says my mother. "Shoot. Hers was only nine feet."

"Girl," says Nicholas to me, "that Duchess of Cambridge ain't got nothing on you."

I hear the sound of footsteps running along the hall outside and Keisha and Teraji, my cousins from New York burst into the room, wearing baby pink strapless bridesmaids gowns that flow to the ground and sway around their ankles. They look so pretty. Like angels.

"Ohmygosh!" squeals Keisha, running up to me and grabbing my hands. "Girl, you look like something out of this world. There ain't no words to describe you right now."

"Yes, there are," says Nicholas. "Try gorgeous, breathtaking, and sizzling."

"Gimme a shot," says Bobby, circling us. "Bridesmaids, could y'all stand on either side of the bride for me?"

Keisha and Teraji come to stand beside me and we all smile for the camera.

"That's good, girls," says Bobby, "love y'all."

"Ready baby?" my mom says, her eyes bright with tears.

I can't speak. I can only nod my head.

I look at myself in the mirror. I look more beautiful than I've ever looked in my life. So why do I feel so uncomfortable? Like something's wrong? Or about to go wrong?

Promise me that if for any reason... any little reason at all... something don't feel right... you'll come to Daddy. Okay, baby?

"Oh, your daddy is gonna die when he sees you," cries my mom, dabbing her eyes. "Ronnie!" she calls, hurrying to the door, "Ronnie! Come see your baby."

My father swings into the room. He looks at me with such awe on his face I know I can't spoil it for him.

✡ ✡ ✡

IT'S SUNDAY AND TRAFFIC is light. The sky is a misty blue, the wind crisp and clean. It's a nice day.

As I speed along the highway on my bike, I

think about Dalvin.

A wise man once said that the evil men do lives after them, while their good is buried with their bones. Shakespeare, I believe. He's right, too.

But I've made up my mind that this evil is gonna die.

✡ ✡ ✡

THE CHAPEL IS FILLED with people, maybe about six hundred. I don't know most of them, but I know that a lot of them are important folks in the city. I stand in the foyer beside my father looking tall and handsome in his black tux, one arm tucked into his, the other cradling my bouquet, which is made of three dozen white roses. My six bridesmaids and Keisha, my maid of honor, are in the foyer too in their pink gowns and matching pink bouquets. Another photographer snaps shots of us. The flashing lights of the cameras are starting to give me a headache and I feel kind of woozy as I listen to the mass choir doing a fabulous a cappella piece. Then the organ strikes up the wedding march.

"It's time," says my dad, that awestruck look still on his face as he looks at me. "You ready princess?"

"Yes," I whisper.

Keisha goes out first, looking pretty and graceful as she scatters pink flower petals along the aisle. The choir hits a high note as my dad and me step out on to the aisle. I hear people gasp at the sight of me in my fabulous gown, and mad cell phones and cameras go off as they take pics of us. D is standing at the altar, Demetrius beside him, in their black tuxedos looking Superstar NBA players. As my father and me walk up the aisle together D stares at me as if he can't believe his eyes. I keep my eyes on him and he keeps his eyes on me. I wonder if he feels nervous like I do.

As we near the top of the aisle, I glance at Mr. Dewitt. His face is serious, like his son's. He gives a little thumbs up to me and my dad as we pass him. Mrs. Dewitt puckers her lips into a little kiss and dabs her eyes. My mom is beside her sobbing into a lace handkerchief. I used to think the crying mother at the wedding was mad corny, but now that I'm going through it, I get it. I know exactly how she feels, cause I wanna cry into my handkerchief too.

As we reach the altar, the chapel goes completely silent except for the soft buzzing of the bees hovering around the flowers in the ceiling, and it seems as if the high arches and the tall pipes of the organ make this occasion even more grand.

"Dearly beloved," says the priest, Father Delaney, our family's spiritual adviser for years. "We are gathered here in the sight of God to unite Dalvin and Mercedes in holy matrimony."

I feel the tears rush up from my heart again, and I fix my eyes on my husband. He looks at me as if he's trying to reach out to me from his soul.

"Marriage was ordained by God in Eden," says Father Delaney, his voice strong and musical. "It is therefore not to be entered into lightly, but reverently, soberly, and in the fear of God."

There's a slight rustling among the congregation. Somebody coughs.

"Who gives this woman to be married to this man?" says Father Delaney.

"Her mother and I do," says my dad, his voice echoing through the quiet chapel.

"Marriage is a joyous occasion," says Father Delaney. "It is connected in our thoughts with the charm of home, and with all that is pleasant and attractive as being one of the most important events of our lives. In its sacredness and unity, it is like the mystical relation between Christ and His Church, and is the most significant and binding covenant known to man.

"Therefore, a man leaves his father and his mother and cleaves to his wife, and they become one flesh. Let every one of you who is a husband love his wife as he loves himself, and let the wife honor and love her husband."

Then R&B Superstar Usher comes from the wings carrying an acoustic guitar and stands behind Father Delaney. A loud gasp comes from the people in the church and mad cameras and phones pop off photos like crazy. Usher strums a melody on his guitar that sounds pure and sweet in the church and the choir hums along. It was all so amazing I felt I was in a dream.

"Do you, Dalvin," says the priest, "standing in the presence of God and these witnesses, solemnly pledge your faith to Mercedes? Do you promise to live with her according to God's ordinance in the holy estate of matrimony? Do you promise to love her, comfort her, honor and keep her, in sickness and death, and forsaking all others, keep yourself only unto her, and through God's grace to promise to be to her a faithful and devoted husband as long as you both shall live?"

"I do," says D.

"The first time ever I saw your face," sings Usher in his clear, beautiful voice, "I thought the sun rose in your eyes. And the moon and the stars were the gifts you gave, to the dark and endless skies my love..."

"Dalvin," says the priest, "do you have a token of your love for Mercedes?"

Demetrius hands the ring to the priest.

"The first time ever I kissed your mouth, I felt the earth move in my hands. Like the trembling heart of a captive bird that was there at my command..."

"Mercedes," says Father Delaney to me, "do you receive this ring in pledge of the same on your part?"

"I do," I say. My hand trembles as D slides the ring on my finger.

"...I felt your heart so close to mine. And I knew our joy would fill the earth, and last till the end of time, my love..."

"Mercedes," says Father Delaney, "do you have a token of your love for Dalvin?"

Keisha, a big nervous smile on her face, hands him the ring.

"Dalvin," he says, "do you receive this ring in pledge of the same on your part?"

"I do," says D.

"The first time ever I saw your face..."

I slip the ring on his finger. His hand feels strong in mine. I look into his gorgeous eyes and feel safe.

"The wedding ring," says Father Delaney, "is the outward and visible sign of an inward and spiritual bond which unites two hearts in endless love.

"The circle, the emblem of eternity, the gold, which cannot be tarnished, is to show how lasting and imperishable is the faith now pledged. Let the ring, a fit token of what is unending, continue to be to you both a symbol of the value, the purity, and the constancy of true wedded love, and the seal of the vows in which you have both pledged your most solemn and sacred honor..."

✡ ✡ ✡

I'VE BECOME TIRED OF shedding blood after all

these years. I'm a professional and I do what I'm paid to do, but it so bores me now.

Of course, Dalvin's blood is special, although according to the terms of Shepherd's oath, not even spilling his blood will break the circle. But I know what will.

I shove aside thoughts of Dalvin, and as I push my bike to its maximum speed, try to think about something more pleasant. Mercedes...

✡ ✡ ✡

"...BY THE AUTHORITY COMMITTED unto me as a Minister of the Gospel of the Church of Christ, I declare that Dalvin and Mercedes are now husband and wife, according to the ordinance of God and the law of the State of Illinois, in the name of the Father and of the Son and of the Holy Spirit, Amen. You may kiss the bride."

The choir bursts into singing again as he kisses me. Everybody claps. He takes my hand. I'm officially Mrs. Dalvin Dewitt. Tons of people come up to us, congratulating us, kissing me, kissing him, hugging us.

We weave slowly through the guests making for the front of the church. When we get to the steps in the cool spring morning, I feel as if my joy is complete. I turn to my husband. He smiles at me, happy and confident. I hear the sound of wings and look up. Hundreds of white doves are released into the sky. I brush away the dark cloud that's been overshadowing my soul.

My mother is fussing over me again, arranging my train around me feet, letting it cascade down the church steps. D and me smile for the photographer from the Chicago Tribune.

"Throw the bouquet, baby," my mom whispers to me, sounding excited.

I look at D and we laugh as I throw the beautiful bunch of flowers up and behind me, not caring who catches it. I'm still kind of in a daze.

"Time to go, doll," says Mrs. Dewitt, and I notice that our custom white Maybach has pulled up at the front of the church to take us to Casa Tranquilo. I'm suddenly very excited. I'm gonna eat cake and drink wine and dance with my husband and party like there's no tomorrow.

I HEAR THE SOUND though it's still far away, and know it's the sound of death. Ronnie Clinton hears it too, and so does my father. They both glance in the direction of the sound, and as he looks around, I make eye contact with my dad. He has that take no prisoners look in his eyes, and my hand reaches for my Glock under my tux. I slide my fingers around the butt, feeling her sit nice and snug in my palm. Demetrius reaches for his gun too.

I look around for Mercedes. She's surrounded by her bridesmaids, her mother is next to her, and guests mill around taking pictures of her with their phones. I see my mother, talking to the Commissioner's wife. They look like a flock of beautiful, happy tropical birds, and for a brief moment, I feel fear—an emotion I'm not used to or comfortable with. I wanna yell at them to run. But the sound is still a far way off, and it might just be some idiot showing off with a suped-up dirt bike.

Then I hear the other sound. It's close. Very close. Like it's right on top of us. My hands fly out in the direction of the sound, my Glock cradled between my palms.

"Get down!" I yell. "Mercedes!" She spins around, confusion and shock spreading over her face as the dirt bike whizzes through the air overhead and hovers over her for a second. The momentum from the jump sends the bike and the rider crashing into a table. Champagne glasses fly into the air in a spray of splinters.

The rider, his body suited down in black leather, his head hidden inside a helmet, steadies the bike with his leg, makes a crazy tight u-turn, and speeds right at me. I aim for his chest and squeeze the trigger of my Glock, bracing myself against the kick as his hand flies out and he fires his gun. I hear the bullet whiz over my head as I drop to the ground and roll out of his way, still shooting. I jump up, my Glock ready. The rider had dropped off his bike, and his body is being trampled by a crowd of screaming people, scrambling to get to safety.

In my peripheral vision, I see my dad, Demetrius, and Jimmy. I see Ronnie Clinton and Maurice, their weapons aimed at another dirt bike as it flies overhead. Their guns go off at the same time and the bike drops to the ground, engine screeching. People scatter, tumble over each other as the rider falls to the ground.

Then they're whizzing into the garden, one after the other, like birds of prey, skidding on to the ground, dropping on to tables, engines screeching. I see more of my father's soldiers and Ronnie Clinton's converging around the bikers. Stephano, his M-9 in his hand, pops one of the riders as he drops down onto the grass, his blood spattering the ground and the people around him. My dad takes aim at another biker and drops him.

More bikers fly into the garden. I see Maurice and Ronnie Clinton take aim and fire. The air is filled with the sound of screeching brakes, people screaming and gunshots.

The bikers keep pouring into the garden. I look around for Mercedes. I don't see her. I don't see my mom either.

The bikes' engines are so loud they drown out every other sound, except the sound of gunshots. They're about fifty of them now, and they keep coming.

IT'S A PRETTY GARDEN. The lawn is huge and very green and neatly mowed. They had arranged pots of flowers and swan decorations all over. I think the swans are a nice touch. I rev up my bike and ride over one of them, mowing down pots of flowers in my path.

I see the wedding guests up ahead. I hear screams and the sound of dirt bikes, and I feel a rare jolt of excitement. The party has started. I'm just in time.

I ride straight into the chaos, weaving in and out of the people, seeing them look at me with terror in their eyes. But I'm not interested in them. I'm looking for my target.

I see him up ahead. The bikers are circling him, and he isn't going down easy. He's holding a semi-automatic pistol in each hand and shooting off a stream of bullets.

I break through the riders and hop off my bike, letting it shoot forward on its own momentum. The old man turns towards me as I roll my AK up to his head and squeezed the trigger. The force of the bullet from my AK causes him to stagger wildly backward. His blood sprays the air around him. He's a tough old dog. He remains on his feet staring at me. Then I see the light go out of his eyes. His pistols fall from his hands. I keep on shooting, the other bikers holding the formation of their protective circle around us, preventing any intervention.

Then Dalvin Dewitt hits the ground. I keep shooting, even though I know he's dead. He ain't that bulletproof.

"Dad!" I can't move. The horror of seeing his torn and bloody body sprawled on the grass is too much to bear. My knees go weak.

"Dad!" His eyes look at the sky. The shooter is still standing with his weapon in his hand, one leg supporting his weight, the other bent at a casual angle, suited up in black leather, looking like a killing machine.

It's blind rage that cause my hands with my gun to fly up. The bullets sound like a raging storm around me. The killer staggers backward. Then one of the bikers turns and comes at me. I shift and fire at him, seeing him fly off his bike. I drop to the ground as his bike whizzes over my head and crashes hard into something behind me. I jump to my feet, my eyes scanning the area for the killer. I can't make him out among the other bikers so I pick up my father's weapon and walk right into the riders, a gun in each hand, firing them both, knowing that one of my bullets will find him.

"Get down, Mercedes!" I hear the raw urgency in D's voice and know it's for real. I look around. He's gripping a huge gun and his eyes are menacing, then he fires at the rider on the dirt bike that flies over me. I fall to the ground. I hear Teraji scream as she falls on top of me, the folds of her gown covering my face, almost choking me.

"Mercedes!" it's my mother, her voice a high-pitched squeal. "Mercedes!"

"Mom!" I cry.

The screeching sound of the dirt bike's tires drowns out my voice. Teraji rolls off me, and I try to get up, but I'm all wrapped up in the train of my dress, and I can't move. Then I hear Maurice. He's right over me.

"I got you, Mrs. Dewitt," he says. He picks me up. "Hold onto me, Mrs. Clinton!" he said then grabbing my mom.

He runs, stumbling with me in his arms. I feel his heart pounding hard as he barges through knots of people. When we reach the villa, Maurice releases me. I stumble on my feet as he pushes open the door and helps me to the sofa. My mother falls onto the sofa beside me.

"Ohmygosh!" I scream, as the full impact of the fear I'm feeling overcomes me. I feel like I'm drowning in it, the fear and the numbness and the feeling of not feeling what I'm feeling. "Ohmygosh! Ohmygosh!" I kept screaming.

"Hush, baby," my mom says, sounding scared.

I jump up, and she grabs my arm and pulls me back onto the sofa.

"No!" I scream, as I fight her off. "D! Where's D?" I tear at my dress, trying to get it off me. But it's a sturdy well-made dress, and I can't rip it. My mother's hands tremble as she turns me around and unzips the dress. I kick off my shoes and scramble out of the folds of the gown's heavy fabric.

"Why?!!" I scream, allowing my fear and anger and frustration and disappointment to flood through me. "Why?! Why?! Why?!"

My mother holds onto my arms and strokes my face with her fingers as the tears roll down her cheeks.

"Hush, baby," she says trying to put her arms around me.

"Where's D?" I scream again, and break free from her and run to the door. It's locked, and I tug and bang on it till my hands hurt, crying and bawling at the top of my voice. I hear the gunshots outside.

"Baby!" says my mother, "you cannot go out there."

"D!" I scream, "I gotta find D!"

"No, baby," says my mother, her fingers strong like iron on my arms. "No, no, you can't go outside."

Then the door gives way and people pour inside. I see Keisha, her dress covered in blood.

"Keisha!" I scream. "You alright?"

But Keisha's so scared, she can't say anything. She falls onto the floor. I go to her and fall to my knees beside her. I realize the blood is only on her clothes, and she's not hurt at all. She so scared, though, she can't stop screaming.

"It's okay, sweetheart," I say. I hold her in my arms and rock her like a little baby till she quiets down.

"LET'S GO, SON." HIS voice seems to come from a far distance. "Get up." But I can't get up. I have to keep him from slipping away from me. I hold on to him, burying myself in his flesh and his blood, trying to keep him from leaving.

"Let's go, D," says Ronnie Clinton again.

"No!" my voice is high-pitched like a girl's. I grab on to my father even tighter.

"Son," says Ronnie, "he's gone."

"No!" I yell at him.

"Yes," he says. He grabs both my hands, pulls me up off my father. I lash out at him in rage, and he staggers back, holding up his arms defensively. He doesn't try to fight me, lets me punch him, holding up his arms as I swing at him.

"It's okay, D," he says over and over. "That's right. Get it out. It's okay, son."

But it's not okay. My father is dead. Things will never be okay again.

Chapter Twelve

Aftermath

I was bored with the television coverage of Dalvin Dewitt's death. Goodness, how they go on and on. I know he was a high-profile candidate for mayor, and was a pretty strong contender too, despite the little smear campaign I started, but do they have to make him into some kind of martyr?

I was amused, though not surprised, to discover what little regard people have for the truth, despite what they say. All you have to do is get yourself a really good spin-doctor, and you can make yourself into whatever or whomever you want. And I have to admit, Ronnie Clinton was good. He was an exceptional liar. No matter how many times I published my ads detailing Dalvin's involvement in every dirty little aspect of organized crime in Chicago, Ronnie would come back with some bleeding heart story about Dalvin's good deeds, his involvement in the community, his sponsorship of this or that charity, his big brother programs, his soup kitchens.

He was so good I found myself starting to admire Dalvin's smooth television personality. He and Ronnie were completely unscrupulous. They did what they had to do and said what they had to say to gain favor with their constituents. And they had all this street aggression that they transferred to the media. They put a whole new spin on hard sell. I even contemplated applying for a job in one of Ronnie's companies. God knows I was tired of Shepherd.

Dalvin's funeral was a who's who of gangsters, both the legit and illicit kind. Ironically, it was held in the same church where his son was married only a few days ago. Now since his death, he's become some kind of hero. Just like my dad.

And these reporters keep going on about how miraculous it was that none of the wedding guests were shot. What's so miraculous about that? We're professionals. We know what we're doing. We aimed for our target and got him. I'm so irritated I want to change the channel, but Jacob and Spider are soaking up the news reports. I take another sip of my beer.

Jacob has been out of the hospital for a while, and he's pretty much back on his feet. His dad is alive too. Their armored truck saved them that day, no doubt.

I look at him sprawled on the couch next to Spider, his eyes fixed on the television screen. He's maybe the same age as D, with that clean-cut Ivy League stamp on him. I know he's upset because his little escapade with Dalvin forced him to drop out of his undergrad program at Duke University, but that was his own fault. He didn't seem to think things through before he did them. He's hot headed. He has definitely not inherited his father's strategic skills.

I know Adam wanted to take Jacob out of the country and come back to deal with Dalvin, and Adam had enough fire power to take out Dalvin and all his soldiers. But D's airborne attack nipped that little plan in the bud. D is so relentless we knew they wouldn't last very long in the hospital. We lifted them out of there just seconds before D walked in.

Jacob flicks his eyes in my direction, and I turn my face to the TV screen. I feel his eyes on me. I can tell he don't trust me.

Logistically, we're getting closer to being able to beak the circle, cause three of us are together now, but in actuality, we might be even further away. There's the little matter of getting these different personalities together in the same room— Dalvin Dewitt, sociopath. Jacob Powers, psychopath. Mercedes Clinton, prima donna.

Then there's the further problem of getting everybody focused on something they probably don't even know about. I'm pretty sure Mercedes has been dreaming. Her reaction to my not-so-subtle suggestion convinced me that she is. Dalvin probably is too, though his super-macho alpha-male personality might prevent him from realizing it. It was hard enough to get Jacob to believe what we were trying to tell him.

But no worries. You can't fight your way through every problem. Sometimes you have to use persuasion. And that's a very useful skill I learned from Shepherd. I'll let Spider work on Dalvin, and I'll continue to work on Jacob and Mercedes.

Chapter Thirteen

Inner Circle

Security is tighter than the Pentagon in Dalvin's building. Not only do I have to strip and go through a scanner at the entrance, when I get up to the fifty-seventh floor where his office is, they did another strip search. Then when I get outside his office, Stephano materializes out of nowhere and frisks me with a wand.

"Nothing personal, man," he says as he passes the wand in front my body.

"Hey," I say, as Jimmy opens the door for me to go in, "gotta do what you gotta do."

D is sitting on the edge of his desk, one leg supporting his weight, the other dangling casually over the side. His eyes are focused on his phone, and I assume he's going through the little slide show I'd sent him.

He looks up as I come in. His eyes are expressionless and rimmed with red, the familiar sign of sleeplessness. I'm well acquainted with that condition.

"Come on in, Spider," he says, slipping off the desk and going round to sit in his chair.

His father's death had taken a toll on him. He looks older. He moves slower and he's limping again, though not so much as before. I'm not surprised. He's had a lot dumped on him all of a sudden. Not only did he see his father gunned down before his eyes—at his own wedding, no less—with his father gone, Dalvin has come into a tidy inheritance and his status within the crime underworld has also changed. He has become the head of the Five Families of the Southside, one of the city's most influential crime cartels. Dalvin Dewitt the Second is now The Boss.

✿ ✿ ✿

"WHEN I WAS LITTLE," she says, "I used to dream about food a lot."

We're in her car, a cool Mercedes Benz convertible, driving along the sixty eight. I'm finally forced to admit to myself that I'm confused, and when it comes to women, I'm never confused. I always know what I want, how I want it and how much of it I want. I never allow myself to be sidetracked by a pretty woman. Most of the girls I know are strippers anyway, and things are usually straightforward with them.

But Mercedes is different. She's a real woman, meaning she's someone you can actually be with. And she's gotten under my skin. I don't even remember when it happened. It might have been the day I saw her up close and personal for the first time in the restaurant with her mother. Or it might have been before that. What I do know, though, is that when I got her call that morning, I felt good. Real good. Said she really needed to talk and that we'll have to drive out of the city 'cause she didn't want D to see us together.

I look across at her. She has a way about her, as if she's trying to embrace every part of you, a kind of uninhibited love of life that's alien to me and I feel I want to experience it over and over.

Her skirt had slid high up her thighs as she manipulated the pedals. Makes me feel like I want to reach over and touch... explore.

Too soon, Rave. Too soon.

I cross my arms over my chest and fix my eyes on the cars in front.

"I dreamed that the sun was a great big pizza up in the sky," she's saying, "and that candy grew on trees." She chuckles. "Then as I grew older, I dreamed about shopping. I'd buy purses and dresses, and... food. I never had nightmares. My dreams were nice, you know? Like entertainment my mind put on for me while I slept until recently."

She's quiet for a long time. As she steps on the gas to pass a car in front of us, I sneak a look at her thighs.

✡ ✡ ✡

I SETTLE INTO THE chair in front of his desk and pull out my iPad. He rests his chin on his knuckles and fixes his eyes on me. I'm familiar with the gesture. It's the calm before the storm.

"Walk me through this," he says, sitting back and glancing at his phone.

In the first photo, a man, his face clean-shaven, his graying hair cropped close to his skull, looks with cool, confident eyes into the camera. He's sporting a leather jacket and a thick gold chain. His arms are crossed over his chest. He looks like a suave, aging model.

"His name," I say, "is Eli Jonas, aka The Shepherd. Originally from Jamaica. Grew up in Queens. Daddy was a preacher, mother worked as a nanny for a Jewish family. Back in the late nineties he moved to Chicago and started a non-profit that helped a lot of folks struggling below the poverty line. He dropped out of sight suddenly, and everybody thought he was dead. When he resurfaced recently, he had become the man you see in the second photo..."

D scrolls to the second photo, showing the wheelchair-bound old man with the patch. He studies the photo, his fingers stroking his chin. He scrolls back and forth between the two photos, looking for a resemblance between the cool-looking able-bodied guy in the first photo and the wheelchair-bound cripple in the second.

"How'd he get like that?" he asks, almost absently.

"He was attacked."

"By who?"

"Your father," I say almost too casually.

He flicks his eyes up at me. They're sharp and penetrating. He looks at the photo for a long time then scrolls to the third photo.

"You know what that is?" I ask him.

He's looking at the photo with interest. Otherwise his face shows no emotion.

"Yeah," he says. "It's an oxygen chamber. They had me in one of those for a little while after they took out my lung."

"Yeah. It's a hyperbaric oxygen chamber. Shepherd sleeps in it at night."

"Like Michael Jackson did," he says and laughs.

"Right. Shepherd really needs his, though," I try not to show any traces of feelings on my face.

The chamber looks like a large capsule made of glass with a dashboard covered with dials and buttons. Shepherd is lying on the mattress inside, his eyes closed, looking like a vampire.

"My father did this to him?" he asks, his voice soft and mild.

"Yes. He did."

D frowns.

"He must have really pissed off my dad to get a beat down like that."

"They had... differences."

D studies the photo for a moment before scrolling to the next one. It shows Shepherd again, strong and able-bodied, along with Richard Stones, Dalvin Dewitt, Ronnie Clinton, Isaiah Jones and Adam Powers.

"That was the inner circle of his organization," I say. "He called it The Brotherhood. Note the tats of the snake eating its tail on the arms of all the men. It's the symbol of infinity. It's the symbol of the Brotherhood."

Dalvin's eyes are fixed on the photo, devouring the image of the six men. It's clear the photo is significant to him. I keep my eyes on him. He's silent for a long time.

"I know this photo," he murmurs. "I seen it among my dad's things."

"Are you aware that your dad was a member of The Brotherhood?" I ask probingly.

He cocks his head as he looks at the picture.

"No."

"He didn't tell you anything?"

He shakes his head.

"The man, the second from the right. That's

my father."

He frowns slightly then looks up at me. I can see the question in his eyes.

"My father, yours, Jacob's, Mercedes'—all members of Shepherd's inner circle of The Brotherhood."

"What's that?" he asks. "Sounds like some kind of... cult, or something."

"It was. It was a combination of the NAACP, the Black Panthers, and the Bloods... within the framework of a non-profit."

He nods. I can see he's familiar with the concept.

"But the inner circle was a kind of secret society. The reason your dad never spoke of it was because he wasn't supposed to. The next photo shows the symbol The Shepherd used in his initiation ceremonies..."

He scrolls to the image of the pentagram.

"If you look at the third photo again, you'll notice that the chamber is sitting in the middle of the same symbol."

He scrolls quickly back and studies the photo.

"It's a symbol that can mean either harmony or conflict, or the resolution of conflict through harmony. Shepherd's version of the pentagram incorporates the elements of earth, water, fire, air, and spirit. Each member of The Brotherhood represented a particular element."

He's silent as he gazes at the image.

"My father was fire," he murmurs.

"How do you know that?" I ask, trying to keep my voice steady.

He looks up at me, and I see he's searching for an answer.

"I... someone told me," he says.

"Who?" I probe trying to keep my composure.

✪ ✪ ✪

"TELL ME," I SAY, glancing at her sideways, admiring the lines and curves of her slender body.

"Well..." Mercedes says, "I don't remember much. I remember... like being in some kind of cold, dark room, like a basement somewhere. I know I'm not alone, but I can't see the other people. Then I see him... parts of him... his legs... he's walking... I didn't know he could walk."

"Yeah," I say, "he can."

"So, he's walking, like towards me... there are lines on the ground... cris-crossing each other... and a big circle... as he comes towards me, he takes off his hat... it... kinda... falls on the ground. He stops walking just as he reaches the edge of the circle... he pulls the patch off his eye... his face is like... a... death head... and I wanna scream, but I can't."

✡ ✡ ✡

"DID THE OLD MAN tell you?" I ask, keeping my voice low.

He looks at me. "How could he?" his voice is sharp. "I never met him." But he's thinking about my question. He shakes his head, as if trying to clear away unwanted thoughts.

"Note the circle on the outside of the pentagram," I continue not wanting to stray away from the ultimate goal.

He looks once more at the image.

"The Shepherd believes that as long as it remains unbroken, he'll live forever."

Dalvin chuckles at this. "Live forever, huh?" he says. "This dude sounds crazy. Looks crazy too."

"Yes, he is."

"Yo man, you believe this?"

"D, I'm a left-brained tech man. I believe in science, in hard facts. But sometimes you see things that defy science."

He shrugs, amused.

"Take Shepherd. He was beaten with the butt of a gun. His skull was smashed in, his ribs shattered, his arms broken so bad one of them had to be amputated. He had so many organs removed he's practically empty inside. He should be dead. And your father should have died after being shot five times by Adam Powers."

He looks up at me again, his eyes steady.

"And you should have died when you were shot by Jacob..."

"What's your point, man?"

"As I said, things sometimes happen that you... you can't explain."

"Like a man surviving a beat down like that?" he asks. "He don't even look like he really alive. He look like he dead on his feet."

"Like a man being able to make you dream certain things," I say.

He cocks his head. "Whadoyou mean?" he asks.

"Do you dream, D?" I ask him. "Do you dream about him sometimes?"

He squints. Trying to remember. "I don't dream," he says finally.

"You don't realize..."

"I. Don't. Dream," he says again, his eyes going hard.

✡ ✡ ✡

"IN THE SECOND DREAM," Mercedes continues, "he speaks to me, asks me something 'bout if I have something. I look in my purse, but it's empty. 'Look. Again,' he says. I look again. And I see it, and I'm mad scared, cause it isn't what the old man is talking about, and I feel that if he finds out I have it, he would kill me for sure."

She puts her hand in her purse next to her, flicking her eyes from the road in front, and stepping on the gas. I quickly remind myself that this whip has some really good airbags. She feels around inside her purse then pulls out a little gun.

"This is what I saw in my purse in the dream," she says, looking over at me, her pretty eyes filled with misery.

"Where'd you get that?" I ask, surprised.

"My dad gave it to me," she says before looking at the road again, "the day after y'all came up to our table in the restaurant."

I almost can't hide my amusement but hold back my laughter.

✡ ✡ ✡

"HERE'S THE THING, D," I say. "It really don't matter if you believe or not. What matters is what you do now that I've told you all this."

"I'm listening," he says, placing his phone on his desk.

"The old man, Shepherd, has to die. We have to kill him."

He's silent. He looks out the glass walls of his office at the skyline beyond.

"We?"

"Me, you, Jacob, Mercedes, and the son of the other Brotherhood member."

"You mean... like a ritual killing?" he asks.

"Yes."

He shakes his head. "No." I notice the note of authority in his voice, how final the word sounds. I push on through anyway.

"Why?"

"First of all," he says, "I don't want my wife involved in anything like that, and second of all, I... I don't have time for cults or ritual killings or anything like that."

"Don't have time? That man is your father's killer."

I see the confusion spread over his face as what I just said sinks slowly in. He doesn't answer immediately.

"No," he says. "No, he's not. I saw the killer." His voice cracks. "I saw him. He was a young dude on a dirt bike. It wasn't this old man."

"Shepherd didn't actually pull the trigger," I say, looking him dead in the eye. "But it was his idea to kill your father."

He rests his chin on his hand. His fingers tremble. He's fighting with his emotions.

"How do you know this?" he says.

"I know."

"Don't you be messing wit me, man," he says, a threat in his voice. "Don't you be messing wit me."

"Believe me, D, I ain't. I wouldn't do that."

"Why would he want to kill my father?"

When a certain kind of man goes all calm in the midst of anger, that's not a good thing. D went very calm. His eyes, riveted on me, are almost mild.

"Shepherd feels your father was a traitor who betrayed The Brotherhood. He thinks your father killed my father. He thinks your father was responsible for the death of Richard Stones. He says your father turned him into the cripple he is now."

D doesn't say anything, but I can see he's rolling over everything I'm saying in his mind.

"Your father had a scar on his hand, right?" I ask.

"Yeah, he does... did."

"Do you know how he got it?"

"It's a gunshot wound. That's all he ever told me about it."

"Shepherd shot him. It's a mark, like the mark God put on Cain, only this mark meant that anyone who wanted to could kill him. Shepherd also put a price on his head."

"Did he? Kill your father?" D questions.

"I don't know. But I would love to."

"What would you do if... if you were to find out he did?"

"The question," I say, "is what would you do."

"If what you say is true," he says, looking at me cool and composed, "you need to tell me where to find this man, so I can speak with him myself. Ask him some questions of my own."

"This is not something you can do yourself. All of us need to do it."

He's silent for so long I thought he'd forgotten about me.

"Spider," he says, in the absent way he speaks now. "I'll think about everything you said." He's looking through the glass wall again, and I knew he'd dismissed me.

"Okay," I say, shutting down my iPad and getting up from the chair. I see no point in arguing with him, at least, not today. Persuasion takes time, and time is one commodity I got a lot of. "You take it easy, D. I'll be in touch." I move quickly towards the door.

"Spider..."

I turn. He's looking at me, and it strikes me that despite the aura of power that surrounds him and the fear with which he's regarded, he's still just a kid.

"Thanks for being honest with me, man."

"No prob," I say, stepping out of his office and closing the door.

Chapter Fourteen

Let Me In

The basement where Shepherd holds his rituals is cold and gloomy. My footsteps echo through it as I approach the pentagram.

Even though I'd been down here many times, the heavy chill still penetrates to my bones. I'm not afraid anymore, though, the way I used to be when I was a kid. It's taken me years to put all that dark matter into perspective, destroy the terror I used to feel, work through the trauma of my childhood, reign in my anger and channel it in the direction I want it to go.

I walk through the circle engraved in the tiles into the pentagram, the same pentagram we see in our dreams.

A master magician can make you believe his well-crafted illusions are real. But when you understand his trade secrets, you'd be surprised how basic it is. I been Shepherd's protégé since I was seven years old, and I'm a committed unbeliever.

As far as the dreams are concerned, he does nothing more than plant suggestions, and dream meditation is a skill he's mastered over the years. It isn't hard. I can do it myself. But if you don't know that it's all an elaborate mind game, it can be pretty scary. I'm aware that Shepherd has been putting some hardcore images in the minds of his sons' children. Some of that stuff is like something out of *The Exorcist.*

I stand in the middle of the pentagram and slowly turn so I can look at each point of the star. Mercedes, Earth. Dalvin, Fire. Jacob, Water. Spider, Air. And me, Rave. Spirit.

The old man has this wild idea he can live forever, and he wants to do it through me.

I walk into the center of the pentagram, sit on the floor and close my eyes. I take a few deep breaths to relax myself.

I'm not gonna let him use me anymore. And I sure wasn't gonna let him devour me.

✡ ✡ ✡

D's grief is deeper than he lets on, and that worries me. I know him. He doesn't let himself get carried away by emotions, and I feel he's slipped into a kind of denial. He misses his dad, but he's trying not to show it. Just like he doesn't like to show when he's in pain. He's taken on so much responsibility lately and hasn't given himself time to rest much.

He's quiet as he finishes his dinner, and his eyes are far away. We moved into his condo for the time being. We still plan to buy a house, but with everything that's been going on, we've put that on hold. We've put most everything on hold.

"Enjoyed your dinner, babe?" I ask him.

"Hmmm?"

My heart sinks. I had fixed a real nice dinner, spread a cute cloth on the table, set the table with pretty plates and silverware and put flowers in the center to make things a little brighter, but he didn't seem to notice anything. Plus he only picked at his food.

I get up and take our plates into the kitchen. It's dark in there, like it is everywhere in the condo. Dark, quiet, and sad. As I rest the plates in the sink, the despair I feel is suddenly so overwhelming, I lean over the sink and just let my tears flow. I cover my mouth with my hands and cry.

I hear him behind me, and I turn on the tap to cover up the sound of my sobs. He comes close and places his hands on my shoulders.

"Mercy," he whispers, bending down and kissing me on the neck. "Mercy, Mercy, I'm sorry."

"Sorry for what, D?" I ask, stifling my sniffles.

He turns me around to face him, and wipes

away my tears with his fingers.

"I'm sorry for... not paying attention," he says, wrapping his arms around my waist. "I'm real sorry, baby."

I wind my arms around his neck.

"I know it's hard for you, D, and I'm tryna be here for you, but you ain't letting me."

He looks down at me with sad, sad eyes as if they're saying, I don't know how to let you in.

I MASSAGE HIS SHOULDERS, pressing my hands down his back where his stress and pain settle. He moans a bit, letting out his pain.

He turns around on the bed and pulls me to him as he lies back on the pillows and holds me tight. I wrap my arms around him and hold on to him. We lie like that for a long time, holding each other. I can feel how much he needs me now.

"I'm here for you, D," I whisper. "I'll always be here for you."

He releases me a little and I snuggle into his chest and shoulders. As he cradles me in his arm, I trace the line of the scar just between his ribs where the surgeon had cut him open to remove his lung.

"Mercy," he says, "I know this ain't what we planned, but we gonna do all the things we planned. I promise."

"We don't have to do those things." I want him to know that none of that would ever change how much I love him.

"Yeah," he says. "We will, baby. We'll go to the Caribbean for our honeymoon just as we planned, and we'll buy our own place. I just have to take care of my dad's estate. And there are a whole lot of other things to take care of. But don't worry. Everything we talked about is gonna happen."

"I know it's gonna be like this for a while. It's okay. I just wanna make sure you're alright, D."

"I'm okay."

"D, you ain't okay. Why do you keep saying you are?"

He doesn't say anything for a moment, and I wonder if he's mad at me. I don't care if he is, though. I'm not going to sit back and watch him work himself to death. And he ain't even eating properly.

"I am okay, Mercy," he's trying to convince himself that what he's saying is the truth.

"Talk to me, D. I'm your wife. Tell me how you feeling."

His eyes are far away, and we just lie in the bed without saying anything for a long time.

"I keep seeing him," he finally says. "My father, his body covered in blood, his eyes... lifeless. I tried to cover him when the bikers surrounded him. I know I took down a lot of them, but they just kept coming. I see the man who killed him, with his gun in his hand. It was an AK. I went after him, but he disappeared among the other bikers. That's all I think about, Mercy. It's like a video that plays itself over and over in my mind. I can't get it out of my head. I can't believe he's gone. I keep thinking he's still here. I keep feeling I'll look around and see him. I miss him, Mercy. I... I never thought he would leave me. I never thought he would die. I always believed he would be with me all the time."

I totally relate, because I feel that way about my daddy too. I don't think he'll ever leave me, that he'll be with me all the time. It occurs to me that I been taking him for granted all these years, and I feel scared suddenly, that he might be taken from me just like that, like how Mr. Dewitt was taken from D, or that D might be taken from me without warning. I can't bear to think about it. I hug D a little tighter.

"I never thought he would die," he says again.

"I know, baby."

"All I want is..."

"Is what, D?"

He's quiet again.

"Today," he says, "I talked to a guy who told me he knows the man who's behind my father's death."

I feel a chill run through me. He squeezes my shoulders, because he feels them shaking.

"Mercy," he says, "do you know that your father was a member of a secret society?"

"No," I say. "My dad never tells me anything, y'know."

He sits up suddenly in the bed and turns to face me.

"Mercy, I'm not gonna do that to you. I know your old man has this misguided idea that he's protecting you by keeping you in the dark. But I think you're safer when you know what's going on. 'Cause when you do, you can defend yourself."

I sit up too.

"I'll never keep you in the dark about anything, baby. You're my wife, and I want you to share my life and everything in it. Okay?"

"Thank you, D," I say, feeling the tears burn my throat and eyes again.

"Your father and my father and Jacob's father were all members of a secret society called The Brotherhood."

"Jacob's father? He knows my father?" I search my memory for the time I dated Jacob briefly while me and D were separated last year. I never felt my father knew him.

"Yeah," he says.

"The Brotherhood? Sounds like something out of a book."

"Yeah, it does. They were blood brothers. Your dad didn't tell you anything?"

"No, I swear."

"You know he has tats, though?"

"Yeah, he has tats."

"And one of them is a snake eating its tail."

"Yeah, I've seen that."

"My dad had a tat just like it. It's the symbol for The Brotherhood."

I feel he's struggling with something he wants to say to me.

"Mercy, you gotta get used to using the gun your dad gave you."

"I am used to it. I got 206 at the range." I'm not trying to sound like I'm boasting or anything, but it comes out that way.

His eyes go hard. "Mercy, shooting a target at the range ain't the same as shooting a real man. I'm talking 'bout shooting a real man."

I knew that's what he meant. And I'm not ready for that.

Chapter Fifteen

Past, Present & Future

He was sitting on a park bench waiting for me. The look he gives me as I approach is far different from the way he used to look at me before my father was killed. His eyes are mellow now, kinder but I ain't feeling all that.

"Hello, son," he says.

"Hi, Mr. Clinton," I say as I sit beside him. He reaches in his jacket, pulls out a leather case and offers me a Cuban. I know it's his way of showing his approval. He says he finally accepts me, but I ain't smiling as I take it and cut off the cap. He leans over to light it, then lights his own, taking a couple deep puffs. He looks around.

"Your dad and me, we used to come here all the time, you know, to talk things out. Strategize."

I don't say anything. I hold the smoke in my

mouth before blowing it out.

"He was my friend," he goes on. "My brother."
He sounds like he's missing my dad as much as me.
"What can I do for you, D?" he asks, not looking at
me.

"Tell me about him. About the Brotherhood.
About Shepherd."

He nods and settles back on the bench, taking
another puff of his cigar.

IT WAS THE SUMMER OF 1995. Things were bad.
Jobs were hard to find, especially if you did time.
Man, when you came out, you couldn't get nothing.
Nobody would hire you. Not even to flip burgers in
a greasy burger joint. Ever heard 'if you're black,
stand back'? It's like they wanted to starve us out.
But they'd give you food stamps, though, after you
stood in line all day at the welfare office. Like they
were punishing you just for being alive.

I spent my days pounding the pavements all
through the South side. I must have went into every deli, diner, laundromat, every retail store ask-
ing for a job. Nothing. In the evenings, I would try
and cop some weed and watch a movie before
heading home. Next day, I'd do the same thing all
over again.

One day, I was kind of wandering through the
South side. I'd spent all morning searching and I was
tired and wondering where my next meal was gonna come from. As I stopped on a corner waiting for

the light, I heard folks singing. I looked around and realized I was standing right in front of a church. I thought someone up there must have heard me. I went in hoping they'd give me a hot meal.

The church was big inside. The walls were covered with pictures of Jesus, all of them black. Black disciples, black Mary, and behind the altar, a big painting of the Lion of the Tribe of Judah. The people singing was the choir rehearsing. They sounded like angels from outta heaven. I sat down at the back of the church.

I must have dropped to sleep. I jumped awake when he sat down beside me. He was the preacher's son. Called himself The Shepherd. Started talking to me about the American Dream and black empowerment and saying that all the stuff Dr. King preached about was ours by right. I was so hungry I don't think I heard half of what he said. I just wanted to get a plate, smoke my blunt, and go home. Then he asked me if I wanted to make some quick money. I said, y'know, yeah—I'm game. It wasn't what I expected, though, breaking and entering, him being a preacher's son and all. But it was easy. I made a cool thousand dollars that very evening, bought myself a big ole steak dinner and some new clothes and was back at that church bright and early the next day.

That was when I met Richard, Isaiah, Adam, and your dad. We went out on another job that very day and almost every day after that. We hit mostly Jews and white folks. Businesses like retail shops. Man, them people were rich. They had so much gold in their houses and money and expensive electronics. Shepherd was a first class fence. He made sure we got paid good. For the first time in my life, I knew what it felt like to have money in my pocket all the time. And not only that, for the first time in my life, I was part of something big and significant. It was called The Society for Black Empowerment. It was a real organization that Shepherd started, but it was also a cover for the illegal things we did.

"DON'T GET IT TWISTED, son," he says, flicking open his lighter and holding the flame up to the tip of his cigar. "Most everything we did was illegal. It was a fact of life. It was the only thing we could do. Our options to make a living was limited."

"So... you weren't concerned 'bout going into the presence of God every Sunday with offerings from your ill-gotten gains?" I ask him.

He thinks about this. "Nah," he says. "A man gotta live. We believed God knew that and understood."

I laugh. What he said wasn't funny, but I was amused.

FOLKS IN THE HOOD believed in Shepherd. He was everybody's godfather and uncle and daddy. The Society for Black Empowerment grew fast.

Most of the members were war vets out on the streets and ex-cons. They didn't have nothing to lose. Shepherd used to say we were the kinda folks Jesus hung out with when he was down here— street people. And helping folks was what we were about. We'd pay your kids' tuition, pray with your grandma, beat the crap out your brother, assassinate your enemy.

We also made a lot of headway in the territories belonging to the Mafia, which was a kind of obsession with Shepherd. He really hated them because they had everyone living in a grip of fear, and he wanted to break their control over us. Of course, when we took over a business, it was just a matter of the owner exchanging one master for another, and The Shepherd wasn't any nicer than The Boss, but our people preferred him to the Mafia any day. He was one of us.

Every day before we went out, Adam, Isaiah your dad, Richard, and I met with Shepherd to plan our moves. Each of us had special skills we brought to a job.

Isaiah—we called him Izzy—was the brains. He knew how to disable any alarm, unlock any door, anywhere. He was the man who got us in, and he could get us into any building in less than sixty seconds.

Once we got in, Richard and Adam moved through like invisible men, never leaving a trace. You would never know they been there. Then when we got everything we wanted, Adam knew how to get us out. He knew every route away from any- where, and he was a crazy man behind the wheel.

Me and Dalvin, we were the ones you didn't wanna meet on your way in or out. If you were un- lucky enough to step into us, we'd put you out of commission for a long time.

We were good. We never made mistakes. Nev- er got caught. That's because we understood each others' moves. We were like five parts of a whole. In sync, you know? We relied on each other to be in the right place at the right time. We had to, 'cause if we didn't have each other's backs like that, it would mean either death or a long time in the slammer. But it was more than that. We respected each oth- er. We were brothers. When Shepherd saw that, he decided to capitalize on it. He may have started the Society for Black Empowerment, but we started The Brotherhood. He just took it to another level.

"WHAT DO YOU MEAN 'another level'?" I ask, thinking about what Spider had said to me.

He smiles and doesn't say anything for a while.

"Shepherd was full of ideas about black folks being God's chosen people and being endowed with special qualities and melanin and dominant genes and all that," he says. "He felt we were spe- cial. He called us his sons. Said the five of us were the five points of the star on which he established his organization, something like how Jesus was the rock on which God established his church. We were the inner circle of his organization. We made it what it was. We were the reason folks feared him and did everything he said. We were his soldiers. His enforcers. His assassins. We were intrigued by his ideas, but none of us went for all the... ritual stuff beyond the fact that it kept us focused."

He went quiet again, and I realize I would have to pry what I want out of him.

"What ritual stuff?" I ask.

He takes his time answering.

SHEPHERD WAS VERY RELIGIOUS, but he was also twisted. He felt he was anointed. And he was into control big time. We used to meet in his basement and take a blood oath, a commitment to him and to each other. He said the oath would make us rich. And we did get very rich real quick.

But we knew we got rich because of demand and supply. Folks demanded drugs, we supplied them. They demanded guns, we sold them. They wanted quick cash, we loaned it to them with interest. And we stole people's money. I mean, money comes from somewhere, right? It don't materialize out of nowhere. He couldn't fool us into thinking some little ceremony made us rich 'cause we were the ones doing all the dirty work. We knew exactly where our wealth came from. And Shepherd understood how money works. He knew about commerce, investment, moving money through the banks. We needed each other, and he devised his little ceremonies to make sure we stayed together.

He didn't have to do that, though. Like I said, the concept of brotherhood came out of the relationship we had with each other—the five of us. In our hearts we were brothers. Not only that, brotherhood meant the difference between life and death to us. One of us stepping out of line even a little meant that all of us could go down. But Shepherd thought all that occult stuff made him powerful. And maybe it did.

"HE THINKS MY FATHER was a traitor." I turn to face him, looking him dead in the eye. I hope he can see I ain't in the mood for no subliminal answers. "Was he?"

"Your father believed in what The Brotherhood stood for too much to betray us," he says. "I believe that with all my heart. You say you wanna know about your father? I'll tell you about him. He was fearless. But you know that. He was a loyal friend. He did right by his friends, and his love ran deep. When he committed to you, he never broke that commitment, but when he was your enemy, you'd think you done died and met the devil himself. And once you became his enemy, you stayed that way for life.

"Me and Dalvin had our differences, but we were never enemies. I'm real glad we were able to save our friendship.

"But I thought about all that over the years, Shepherd's accusations. I have no way of knowing for a fact that D didn't sell us out, but in my heart, I don't think he did. And I had a long time to think about it."

THE STREETS OF CHICAGO breed all sorts of low-life. At the bottom of the food chain are snitches, people that sell information for protection.

One such bottom-feeder was a sly old dog named Carter, who acted crazy, but wasn't really crazy. Carter never washed, he walked around with his hair looking all wild, talking foolish to everybody.

One day he comes to us and says he knows about a heist the Mafia was planning to pull off. They're gonna rob a bank, he says. We didn't believe him, but we knew he had a way of slipping through the cracks like a cockroach. So Shepherd tells him to keep an eye on what the Mafia was doing and keep us in the know.

Turns out the Mafia did rob the bank. They got away with a cool five million dollars. Carter came back to us all full of himself, saying he knows where the money is, and if we wanna know we gotta pay him. Shepherd pays him and he gives us the exact location of where the money was. It was in a safe house on the West side.

Thing is, after the robbery, the cops got on everybody's case and put the streets on lockdown.

The police chief, a man by the name of Hawkes who was trying to become mayor of Chicago, declares a war on organized crime and put undercovers on every street corner. He started picking up a lot of small-time hoods off the streets and shaking them down and making examples of them, but he couldn't touch the Mafia or the Brotherhood.

So Shepherd tells us to wait till after the dust settles a bit, and after that, we would relieve the Mafia of their stash.

Meanwhile, we watched that house day and night, checking out everyone who came and went. Izzy put a tap on their phones, and he also put cameras inside so we could keep track of everything they did. They were so cocky they didn't anticipate much of a challenge from anybody, so they conveniently left open a small window of opportunity for us.

We noticed that two of the four men who stayed in the house usually left at 9:30 every Sunday morning to go to Mass, leaving only two men inside. Maybe they thought some magical fairies would help them guard their stash.

It was only a small window, but it was enough for us. The church was five minutes away, which meant that if the guys inside called them for backup they could be there in five minutes. And we factored in backup from other places. We knew exactly where the money was. We planned it so we could be in and out of there in four minutes flat.

"Y'ALL WERE THAT GOOD, huh?" I say.

"Yeah," Mr. Clinton says, "we were. We'd done it hundreds of times. We coulda done that job with our eyes closed. Turns out, that's exactly what we did."

THE WE DECIDED TO HIT at ten in the morning. Daylight robberies can be tricky, but we had a lot going for us. First of all, it was a quiet neighborhood, mostly Italian Catholic. That time of the morning, most everybody would either be in church or sleeping off the night's indiscretions. Second of all, we been scoping that house for a long time, and we knew how it was laid out inside and outside. There was no reason why anything should go wrong.

I usually went in first, with Izzy right behind me, then Richard and Adam, with D as the rear guard.

Izzy got us in, and we headed for the second floor where the money was. It was easy. I remember thinking at the time that it was too easy, and just as I was wondering where the two guards were, they started shooting. We were ready for them, though. What we weren't prepared for was the other men that started pouring into the hallway. Man, it was a bloody mayhem. Izzy went down, and so did Richard and Adam. We had to pull back, and barely got out of there, don't ask me how. Only three of us made it to the car—me, your father, and Adam, and all of us were hurt and bleeding.

Shepherd went crazy when we got back to his house. Kept screaming 'bout the money. Wanted to know where the money was. His money. 'Where's my money?' That's all he kept saying. That's all he cared about. He didn't care about Izzy or Richard. Didn't care that D, Adam, and me were shot and bleeding. He didn't care about us. All he cared about was the money. Then he started going on 'bout how we been set up, and we were, that was clear. Thing is, by who?

Next day, Shepherd got a phone call, saying to look in the alley at the back of Adams Road. We found Izzy. He was dead, five bullets in his head. We also found a box with Richard's hands in it. Then we got another call, saying if we didn't give them back their money, we'd get Richard bit by bit in parts. But we didn't have their money. We didn't know where it was, and no one else did either. The Mafia was true to their word. They did send us back Richard in parts. First, they sent his feet, then his legs and then his head, minus the eyes. It was the most gruesome thing I ever saw.

"AND SHEPHERD THOUGHT MY father was responsible for that?" I ask. "Why?"

Mr. Clinton thinks about my question.

"Shepherd and your father didn't get along," he says. "Shepherd didn't like him. D was crazy, and Shepherd couldn't get into his head."

"Get into his head?" I say, thinking about Spider again. "How you mean?"

"Shepherd was into control like I said. He watched your every move, and D wasn't always where he was supposed to be. And he was openly scornful of the oaths and rituals. They used to get into fights, mostly about D's attitude to Shepherd. But whatever D felt about Shepherd, he was loyal to us. He wouldn't have let Richard die that way. But none of that changed the fact that we were set up."

THAT WAS THE FIRST time we made a mistake on a job, and it was a mistake that cost us a lot. It cost us two of our brothers, and it cost us the trust we had among ourselves. Shepherd never let up on D, 'cause like I said, they didn't like each other.

Then one night, D confronts Shepherd about the things he was saying, tells him he don't answer to nobody, not even him. Shepherd goes ballistic, talking 'bout how D was the one that set us up. D pulls his gun, threatens to kill him. Shepherd pulls his gun too and shoots D. The bullet hit him in his hand. Shepherd starts talking crazy 'bout how that bullet wound is the mark of Cain, and how it marks D as a traitor forever and how D is sentenced to death.

That was when D went psycho. He swung at Shepherd with the butt of his gun, and didn't stop swinging. He beat him so bad that when me and

Adam found him, he was lying in his own blood, nearly dead. We took him to the hospital and they put him on life support, said he would never recover. He did recover, though, and The Society for Black Empowerment continues up to this day. But the heart of it, The Brotherhood, disappeared. So did Shepherd. So did D.

Adam and me searched all over for D. We searched for months, but we couldn't find him. When we finally found him, Adam walked right up to him and pumped five bullets into him. That was the extent that our trust was shattered. We were turning against each other, killing each other.

I watched as they scraped my brother off the street. I was with them when they took him to the hospital. Stayed with him the whole time he fought for his life. I wasn't gonna let him die too.

I think a lot about the events that broke apart the good thing we had. There was never anything like The Brotherhood again. We were unique. What we had was special. But it was over. I let Adam slip out of my life. D and me quarreled over some minor thing and I just stopped talking to him. I couldn't help wondering over the years if there was more to Shepherd's rituals than any of us realized.

"WHAT WERE THE RITUALS like?" I ask.

He looks into the mists of time again.

"We met in his basement. We each had a word that identified us, and that corresponded to a point on the pentagram. Shepherd always stood in the center. We'd identify ourselves by those names before stepping onto our own point on the pentagram. The ritual was very short. We'd pledge secrecy about what we did and loyalty to Shepherd and each other. That was basically it."

Mr. Clinton rolls up his sleeve. His arm is covered in scars and tats. He points to one of the tats, an inverted triangle.

"This is the symbol that corresponds to my name. The element of earth."

I nod. My father had one of those too. His was a right-side up triangle. Fire.

"It seems that as long as we went along with Shepherd, things went well, but from the time we started to have differences, chaos came into our lives. Chaos and death, and the chaos has trickled down to you. Jacob shooting you, that was Shepherd's influence.

"Son, I now know that we were involved in some pretty hardcore occult stuff. We kind of knew that at the time, but chose not to take it as seriously as we should have. We were more focused on the practical things, the money and all the things money can buy, including fear and respect, and in the hood, there isn't a whole lot of difference between the two. But Shepherd, he was into power. He used us, and we let him."

"Do you ever dream about Shepherd?" I question.

"Dream?" Mr. Clinton says, and chuckles. He doesn't say anything for a while, and I thought he wasn't going to answer me.

"If anyone else asked me that," he says as if he's carefully choosing his words, "I would have said no. But it's you, D. You my brother's son, so I'm gonna be straight wit you. Yeah. I dream about him. I dream about him all the time."

"Do you think my father did?" I wonder.

"I know he did. I think that's why he turned against Shepherd. He wanted to break his control over him. I think that's why they tried to kill each other."

"Is that how you break the old man's control over you? By killing him?"

"Yeah," he says. "But it's not easy to kill Shepherd. He back in full force. He might be a cripple in a wheelchair, but he's very powerful. And he has some mean mercenaries doing his dirty work now."

"How do you know that?"

"I've been following his work. It's all over the news. I'm pretty certain it's them that crashed your wedding. And it looks like he has an assassin. This guy works solo. He's very professional. His work is clean, like how ours used to be."

"Do you know who he is?"

"No," Mr. Clinton says shaking his head, "but if you ever find out who he is, you'll have found your father's killer."

"I met Izzy's son."

"When?"

"The first time was a few months ago. Goes by the name Spider. Tech man."

"Like his dad." He chuckles. "I met Richard's son."

"When?"

"About a month ago. Looks a lot like Richard, but ain't nothing like him. Richard had a heart. This guy is cold-blooded."

We look at each other.

"D, I think your father knew Shepherd was after him."

"What makes you say that?"

"I think that's one of the reasons he persuaded me to give you my blessing to marry Mercedes."

"Excuse me?"

"He persuaded me to let it happen." He looks at me, his face serious.

"I see."

"I think he did that because... he knew Shepherd was stalking him and he didn't want... he didn't want you to be fatherless. He was prepared for anything. He put his house in order. That's why your ascension to the head of the Five Families went so smoothly."

"You could be right." I think about everything Mr. Clinton said to me, trying to put the pieces together in my mind.

"Ever found out who set y'all up?" I ask him.

"Nah. Never. It's been like an itch I can't scratch

all these years."

He sits beside me, puffing on his cigar, not saying anything. For the first time since I met Ronnie Clinton, I felt I could trust him. I knew he was a friend I could count on.

"Thank you," I turn and say.

"For what?"

"For being straight wit me."

We sit like that for a while, both of us in our own private thoughts.

"What's on your mind, Dalvin?" I hear him say.

"Shepherd."

"What about him?"

"If he was the one behind my father's death, I have to make him pay for that."

He nods. "You can't fight him like how you'd fight any other man," he says. "He's a warlock. You gonna need help."

"Yeah. That's what Spider said."

"He's right."

"Says we all have to do it."

Ronnie Clinton thinks about this.

"For as long as I knew The Shepherd, he's surrounded himself with bodyguards whose only job is to take down anyone who comes near him. He's the most paranoid SOB I ever met. You'll need get past whoever he has near him now. You'll have to go into his sanctuary. You'll have to go straight to his soul. You're gonna need my help. I'm here for you, son."

"Thank you, sir, I appreciate that," I say getting up from the bench.

As I walk through the park, I pull out my phone and make the call.

"What up, D," his voice comes through my ear-buds.

"Spider, I thought about the things you said. I'm in."

Chapter Sixteen

Don't Leave Me

Tai Chi. It's a nice, quiet kind of exercise. It tones up the legs and the arms and works on the core. It's relaxing, too. And it goes great with cardio exercises like Zumba.

This move is called the white crane spreads its wings. You cross your wrists, move them up, then open your arms. Move your arms slowly in sync then hold the pose. It looks easy, but it takes a lot of concentration. I'll do the hand strums the lute, and grab the bird's tail, and then I'll go start dinner.

Things weren't exactly back to normal, but they're better. We're still in the condo, and I have been doing a lot of decorating. I put up new light summer shades, changed the carpet, and reuphol-stered the couch. The place looks bright and airy now, and it doesn't feel so depressing. I think D likes it, too. He seems happier, but I know it will be a long time before he's his old self. Meantime, I'm trying to make sure he's eating properly and getting enough rest.

I'm disappointed, though. It's not how I envisioned our life to be. I'm alone most of the time, 'cause D's out working and when he comes in, he doesn't talk to me like he used to. I know he's tired and misses his dad, but he doesn't have to keep shutting me out. It hurts. Most nights we make crazy love, but then when it's over, he shuts me out again and I lie beside him and I cry like how my mother cries back home.

I so understand her now, why she lives the way she does. There's a reason she keeps to herself. She doesn't really have a choice. Every time she goes out, she's surrounded by bodyguards. She's always at risk of being shot at, kidnapped or even worse, killed. No wonder she doesn't have any friends. How could you drag someone into all that? That's why I never see Keisha anymore. Ever since D got shot, her parents didn't want her a round me. They feel she would get herself killed just being in my presence and she almost did, on what was supposed to be one of the happiest days of my life... my wedding.

Is this what my life is going to be like? Shut up in here by myself? I can't go shopping all day every day. Thank goodness I have school. Four different schools accepted me, but I chose the U of Chicago because I didn't want to move out of state away from D. I wonder, though, if I should have chosen a different school, like my dad said, maybe somewhere in a foreign country.

But I don't tell anyone that I'm second-guessing myself, because this is the choice I made. My parents tried to warn me and I didn't listen. I was so crazy about D, I just walked right into this, this tight little box, like Rave said.

I don't know how long he was standing there. I look around and was so surprised, I jump.

"D! I didn't hear you come in. How long were you standing there?"

"Not very long."

He comes and stands beside me.

"That move, it's nice. And if you do it like this..." his hands fly out real fast... "it's even nicer."

I couldn't believe it. D just turned a nice quiet peaceful move into a killing move.

"Of course," he says, "when you do that, he's gonna do this..." he shows me a defensive move. "then you could do this... or this... or this. And if you really quick, you can also do this..." he pulls his gun from his jacket.

I'm completely taken off guard. I can't believe it. I just can't believe what I have just seen. His eyes are on me, and he sees how distressed I am so he pulls back.

"Sorry," he says, coming towards me. He tries to put his arms around me, but I push him away.

"I'm sorry, Mercy," he says. "Really."

"I can't believe you, D," my voice is shaking. "Don't you think about anything but fighting and killing people? Is everything about death with you?"

He spreads his hands. "Sorry. But it's what I do."

"What?" I holler. "Killing people? Killing people is what you do?"

He looks at me. His eyes had gone cold. He seems distant, like a stranger.

There are times I wonder who my husband is. Sometimes I feel I don't know him, like he's someone I never knew. I'd be talking to him and he'd turn into a different person just like that. A stranger. Then he'd switch back to my D again. It's like he's two different people. Like Jekyll and Hyde. It's like I'm married to two different men.

MAYBE I'M MISSING SOMETHING. I don't get how everything's so different with Mercy. When I'm in the office or out with my boys I don't miss nothing. I always know who I'm dealing with and my instincts are always on point. I don't understand how I can make a mistake like this with my wife. I'm always making mistakes like this with her.

I mean, she's only just starting to get used to a new way of life, in a new home away from her parents. Why'd I have to go and pull that move on her? I mean, I know why—I want her to be ready for anything, anytime. Who would have thought that my father would have been murdered at our wedding? It could easily have been me or her or any other member of our family. Why can't she see this? And why is she screaming like that? I can't stand the sound of it.

"Why are you yelling at me, Mercy?" I ask her, trying real hard to keep my voice quiet. "You knew who I was from the time we started dating. I never lied to you about what I do. You agreed to this."

"I know," she says. "But I..."

"What?" I say, feeling annoyed. "You want me to treat you like your father does? Like you a kid? Keeping you in the dark about everything? Pretending that things aren't what they really are? Well, I'm not gonna do that."

"What are you talking about, D?" she screams. "You never talk to me!"

"Well, what do you expect me to talk about?" I yell back. "The latest styles in the mall? 'Cause that's all you ever talk about."

"I wanna talk about other things, D. We used to talk about all kinds of things before. Now you never say nothing."

What does she want me to say? 'Hey, Mercy. Today I popped a guy?' My dad had this problem too. But he solved it by just keeping things on the surface. My father and mother hardly ever spoke of anything significant, except when they went out together to a play or a club or some kind of social event. Then they'd talk about the night they had. But my mother knows how to keep herself occupied.

"This is my life and if you don't like it..."

"If I don't like it what, D?" The tears are flowing down her face and she's screaming like a crazy woman. "What D! If I don't like it what?!! What?!!"

HE'S JUST STANDING THERE, looking at me, stone cold.

"If you don't like it, you can always go back to Daddy and Mommy," he says. "Nobody's forcing you to stay here. But I'll tell you this... if you walk out that door, don't come back. You know why? 'Cause I'm not gonna take you back. I'm not gonna have you walking in and out whenever you feel like. Either you're with me or you're not."

"Walking in and out?" I scream.

"Stop yelling at me, Mercedes," Dalvin's voice is calm, but I know he's fed up because he dropped the cute nickname he calls me.

"Well, you stop pulling a gun at everything!" I holler.

"Stop yelling," Dalvin says again.

"Stop killing people!" I scream.

"Tell that to your daddy."

"Shut up!" I scream. "Shut up! Shut up!" I can't stop screaming. "Shut up! Shut up!"

Then his arms are around me and I'm holding him tight and I'm shaking and screaming.

"Baby, baby, baby," I whisper the words and massage her head as she bawls like a little baby.

"Don't cry, baby," I say, "Don't cry like that." I wish I could cry like that. I envy her ability to just bawl out her pain. I can't reach my pain. It's stomped down so hard and deep it can't never be found, though I feel it all the time. It's in my head. It's in my heart. It's in my body. It's in my soul. At times I feel like I'm nothing but a walking mass of pain.

His voice cracks, and I remember suddenly that he's still grieving for his father. All this time I've been trying to be strong for him, and I can't even be strong for myself.

"I'm sorry," I say. I reach for my towel and blow my nose. "I'm sorry, D. I'm okay."

He looks into my face. I can see he's worried about me.

"I won't do that again," he says. "I won't bring any... anything like that around you again."

"No, D. I wanna know. I need to know. I do need to know how to defend myself. If I had known how to do that, I would have been able to fight Jacob that night..." I see his face go hard as he remembers that night too. "And I like the move. It's... interesting. Did you know how to do Tai Chi?"

"Nah, I don't know Tai Chi, but I do know ten different ways to kill a man with my bare hands."

I feel my face register the shock. "Ten ways? With your..."

"Yeah," he says.

"How'd you learn to do that?"

"Some of it I learned on my own. Some of it my father taught me."

"Your dad taught you how to kill a man with your bare hands?"

"HE TAUGHT ME HOW to defend myself, Mercy," I say to her, "no matter who's coming at me, okay? Thing is, when a man is fighting for his life, he'll come at you with everything he's got. You better have a killer instinct."

"What is it like to kill somebody?" she wanted to know.

I'm shocked by her question. Maybe because it's such a personal question. I've never shared that with anybody, cause it's the dark side, and nobody don't ever talk about that. It's taboo, even among other men who've stepped over into the dark side. It's taboo 'cause the dark side is taboo. How a man deals with his demons is his business. Then you always have to watch out for snitches and other such low life. It's like you're walking a tightrope between twilight and pitch darkness. It's like you've signed a contract with the devil and every minute of your life you expect him to call in his favors.

I look at my wife. At her innocence, her goodness, her beauty, and I understand why her father wanted to preserve it. I'd promised him that I wouldn't put her in any danger and that I'd take care of her. I wasn't going to break that promise.

"When you kill a man you're never the same again. That's why as long as I'm alive, Mercy, you'll never ever have to do that."

"I'M SORRY, D. I'm sorry for screaming and crying. I'm just... tired."

"Yeah," he says, smoothing down my hair and stroking my face. "You need to get more sleep."

"You need to get more sleep too, D. We both need some rest. Maybe we can take a holiday, huh? What do you say?"

"I can't. I'm busy."

"You always busy, ain't you?"

"Yes, Mercy. I am. We'll go away, but not now."

"When?"

"I don't know."

"Well, you know what?" I say, making up my mind real quick. "I'll go away by myself. Right now! I'll pack my things and go away. And you know what? I'm not coming back, 'cause you just said you don't want me walking in and out. So I'll just stay out."

I pull myself away from him, but he grabs my arms and pulls me back.

"Don't walk away from me, Mercy," Dalvin says. His voice is hard and cold, and so are his eyes. "All I said is that we can't go on a holiday. Why is that such a big deal? Why don't you grow up?"

He's holding me so tight, he's hurting my arms. I struggle to get out of his grip. "Let go of me, D," I bark.

But he doesn't let go. He just grips me tighter. It's happening again. He's turning into that other man. The stranger I don't know and don't like.

"Please let go of me," I say, feeling the tears pricking my eyes again. "Let go of me. Please. Please." I struggle hard against him. His hands grip me like iron. His eyes are on me, steady and cold. Suddenly, I'm afraid. I'm afraid of him because whoever this guy is, he ain't D. I keep on fighting to get out of his grip. Then he picks me up and walks over to the couch. He dumps me on it and throws himself on top of me, pinning me down, just like Jacob did. I scream.

"Listen to me, Mercedes." His eyes are dark full of rage. "I want you to stop behaving like a baby, okay? Stop screaming. Stop crying. Stop throwing tantrums. I'm not your daddy. You can't control me like that."

I squirm and struggle under him. "Get off me!" I scream. "I hate you!"

I see the surprise in his eyes. He releases his grip on me a little and I lash out at him, hitting him in the face. He grabs my hand. "Stop that," he says, grabbing my hand again.

I CAN'T BELIEVE SHE hit me. I'm not gonna hit

her back, though. I have never hit a woman in my life, and she's not gonna be the first. My father treated my mother like a queen. He never hit her. But she never drove him crazy either.

I have never seen Mercedes like this. I don't know this person. She's looking at me like she can't stand me or something, or like she's afraid of me and her screaming is really getting to me. I let go of her and stand up, looking down at her on the couch while she curls into the fetal position away from me crying and sobbing. Then she gets up, limps past me into the bedroom, and slams the door.

I throw myself onto the couch. I'm tired and pissed. I wish I could turn back the hands of time, put everything in reverse. I'd walk in that door and when I see her there doing her Tai Chi, looking all fresh and pretty, I'd just say, 'Hey baby. I'm home.' 'Cause it ain't that deep. It don't ever have to get that deep.

Then she comes out of the bedroom. She's in jeans and a camisole top, with a duffle bag slung over her shoulder. I don't say anything. I just watch her as she walks past me out the door.

Chapter Seventeen

No More Tears

"May I have your name, miss?" the man asks standing at the gate.

"It's Mercedes," I say as I look up at him through my car window. "Mercedes Dewitt."

"Do you have an appointment?"

"No, but he's a friend of my family. He knows my father very well."

The suit didn't seem to find anything strange about this. He turns away from me to put a call through to the house. Then he opens the gate for me and I drive inside.

The front door opens before I get to it. A butler takes my coat and escorts me inside.

It's like a palace in there. The foyer is huge and made of polished marble with two enormous winding staircases leading up to the next floor. A tall totem pole stands in the space between the two staircases. The walls are made of mirrors which make the place look bigger and which reflect the statues the old man had all over the place. I hear the whirring noise of the old man's wheelchair and turn to face him.

"Mrs. Dewitt!" He smiles widely, as if he's very happy to see me. "To what do I owe the unmitigated pleasure of a visit from you? Please join me in the den."

I follow him into the inner room. He waves his hand in the direction of a wing back chair and I sit in it, crossing my legs.

"What can I offer you to drink?" he says. "I got juice—organic—and I have organic tea and coffee too. Or maybe you'd like something to nibble on. I have cake."

"No, thank you. I'm fine."

Believe me when I say that I gave the idea of coming to Shepherd's house a lot of thought. My gut is telling me he's responsible for the problems I'm having with D. He's gott into my head and he's gotten between me and my husband.

But however I twisted it around in my mind during my sleepless nights at my parents' house, the idea seemed dangerous and stupid. Like something I shouldn't do, but why should I think it's stupid? It wouldn't seem stupid if D did it or my father. They'd walk right in there, feeling no fear and pop that old man and no one would stop them.

"Does your father know you're here?" asks the old man, as if he was reading my mind. "Or your young husband?"

"No."

"Oh, so you came of your own free will?" he says, sounding delighted. "I'm flattered, Mrs. Dewitt, that a beautiful young lady like you would want to pay a visit to an old man like me. I hope you find your visit worthwhile. How can I help you?"

He looks at me as if he might know what's on my mind.

"I... I've been thinking about you..."

"Once again," he says, bowing his head a little, "I'm flattered."

"...because I know you know my father..."

"Ronnie? Yes, I do. I know him very well."

"...and I know you were... close... once."

"Yes, we were. Ronnie was like a son to me. Regrettably, all that has changed now."

"Y'all belonged to something called The Brotherhood."

"Yes," the old man confirms. "Did he tell you about it?"

"No. Not much anyway."

"Would you like to know about The Brotherhood?" he asks.

"Yes, I would like very much to know about it."

"Well," he says, looking up at the ceiling and blinking his eye. "We were a bunch of thieves."

He burst out laughing, "We stole from the rich to give to the poor. Us. We were the poor. You're very fortunate, young lady, never to have experienced the kind of hopeless, grinding poverty your father knew when he was your age. Your father, however, was a very good thief, as was your late father-in-law. In fact, they were both so good, they ended up stealing from me."

"I know my father has a criminal background," I say, looking at my hands.

"Background?" he says, sounding like he's about to burst out laughing again. "He's a dyed-in-the-wool career criminal. Still is. I'm sorry. There's no other way to put it. I'm glad to see that you've chosen a different career path, though. You go to school, do you not?"

"Yes, U of Chicago."

"And your major is..."

"Finance."

"Ah, an excellent field. If you like, I can advise you on ways to run a business, make money, things like that. Making money is one of my God-given gifts, you know. Ask your father."

I hear the front door open.

"Ahh," he says, "I suspect that's my protégé." He presses a little button on the dashboard of his wheelchair. "Martin... tell Mr. Stones to join me in the den, please?"

"Mr. Stones isn't only my protégé, you know, Mrs. Dewitt. He's also my attorney," the old man informs me. "Brilliant young man with a great future in whatever field he chooses. Unfortunately, he has authority issues, like so many young men today. They don't submit as easily as they should to the leadership of their elders."

There's a soft knock at the door before it opens. Rave comes into the room dressed in a black suit, his hair brushed back in a ponytail and carrying a neat little briefcase in his hand. He looks at me, and for a second, I see a flicker of surprise on his face. Other than that, no one would ever guess we know each other.

"Mr. Stones," says the old man, "this is Mrs. Mercedes Dewitt. Mrs. Dewitt, my protégé, Raven Stones."

"Hello," says Rave, stretching out his hand. "I remember seeing you at the restaurant with your mother, although we weren't introduced."

"Yes. Nice to meet you," I say, noticing how firm his handshake is.

"Same here," he says.

"Mr. Stones, Mrs. Dewitt has paid this old man a visit to acquaint herself with a little bit of history."

"I see," says Rave, not looking at me.

"I was telling her that her father was very good at the work he used to do for me." He laughs again, a really nasty laugh.

Rave looks at him, his face completely blank.

"Well, that will be all, Mr. Stones," says the old man. "I want you to stay for dinner. They're a few things I'd like to discuss with you."

"Sure," says Rave. "Again, it was nice to meet you, Mrs. Dewitt. Will you be staying for dinner too?"

"Oh, please do," says the old man eagerly.

"I'm afraid I can't," I lie. "I... I need to go home and prepare dinner for my husband."

"Ahhh yes!" says the old man. "That quickly I had almost completely forgotten you're a new wife with a number of obligations to your young husband." He flashes a strange look at Rave. "I hope you're enjoying your new estate of wedded bliss, Mrs. Dewitt. I know some people find it... delightful."

"Yes," I say, looking at my hands again.

"Enjoy the rest of your evening... Mrs. Dewitt," says Rave.

"Same here," I say, not looking at him as he leaves the room and closes the door quietly behind him. Suddenly I'm afraid without knowing why. I had seen Rave with the old man on more than one occasion, but actually being in their presence was unsettling. There's a strange thing going on between them, an underlying kind of battle. I couldn't help feeling that beneath all that courteous stuff they really hate each other. I glance up at the old man and realize he's been watching me out of his one eye for a while.

"Okay," he says. His voice is soft. "Cut the crap, young lady. Why are you really here?"

"I told you..."

"Yeah," he says. There's a harsh edge to his voice. "I know what you told me. But why are you really here? You didn't come all this way to ask about The Brotherhood. Your father could have told you about that. And so could Raven. Yeah, yeah. You know each other. Please don't insult my intelligence by pretending you don't. Raven might be a good liar, but you sure aren't."

"I'm sorry... I..."

"And you know what else?" he says, his voice soft and malicious. I knew it was time to get out of his presence, but I just sit there, like an idiot.

"He's in love with you," says the old man, sounding gleeful. "And you're in love with him, too. Oh don't try to deny it. I've observed you two together for some time since you left your husband. Shame on you, Mercedes, stepping out on young Dalvin like that. I thought there was more to you, but turns out you nothing but a skank. Marriage to a Dewitt isn't what you thought it would be, is it? He's not a very nice guy, is he? He's selfish, don't care about your feelings, and there's all this stuff going on that you don't understand. Well, that's because you married a criminal, my dear. One that's spiteful and vindictive and vengeful."

I felt the tears pricking my throat as I listened to the old man, knowing that he's right. Knowing that I knew that about D, always knew it. My parents tried to warn me, and I didn't listen. I know D loves me, but there's a barrier between us that we can't get through. And that barrier is there because of what he does. Now it's worse since his dad was killed. He just shuts himself off from me. I can't get through to him.

And, yes, he's right about how Rave feels about me. We've been meeting over coffee and talking, and I've been kidding myself thinking it's all just a friendly thing. Rave doesn't know how many times I almost gave in to him. The only reason I didn't is because I really want my marriage to work. I'm confused. So very confused.

"I know, I know," continues the old man. "You try your best. Nice dinners, nice home. Giving up your body night after night. But you can't make a dent in his emotions. That's because he has a blood lust. Like his father. You know what that is, right? He likes to see blood being shed. And he likes to do the shedding. And he really likes it, for its own sake. There's nothing you can do about it, my dear. He was born with that curse."

The old man laughs his nasty laugh again, and I swallow my tears. What would my mom do if she were where I am now?

"You don't know anything about my husband and me, Mr. Jonas, or should I call you The Shepherd," I mock. "For your information, we're happily married and as for your suggestion that I have any feelings for your protégé, you're way off base, you liar. As for me being unhappy? You got all the money in the world, the biggest crib on the block, and you the most miserable human being I ever set eyes on. You nothing but an ugly, lonely, old man. And you know what? You'll die a lonely old man because nobody nowhere don't wanna be with you."

I get to my feet. "It was wonderful to make your acquaintance, Mr. Jonas. Do enjoy the rest of your day."

"You enjoy yours, too," he says, sounding smug, as I swing round and walk out of the room. Rave is standing a little way down the hall. He looks up at me as I walk past him.

"You okay, Mercedes?" he questions softly.

"I'm fine, thank you, Mr. Stones," I say and continue on past him to the foyer. The butler seems to materialize out of thin air. I take my coat and strut out the door into the sunshine.

BAD IDEA. BAD, BAD idea. I'm still shaking after my conversation with Shepherd. The tears roll freely down my face. I step on the gas. My phone rings. I glance at it and see his number. I ignore the call. I don't know what possessed me to go there. I must have been crazy.

My phone rings again. It's him. I answer it.

"Mercedes," his voice on the other end is cool. "You alright?"

"Yeah, Rave," I say. "I'm alright."

"You don't sound alright," he says.

"I'm okay, really," I say, holding back a sob.

At this point I'm sick of myself and the endless amount of tears I continue to let flow.

"Remember what I said to you that day in Starbucks? About the walls closing in on you and needing to talk?"

"Yeah, but I can't talk to you, Rave."

"Yes, Mercedes, you can. You really can."

I don't say anything, 'cause I'm feeling more confused than ever. I wanna talk to him, but I don't think I should what with everything I'm feeling.

"Can I meet you somewhere?"

"When?" I ask, embarrassed because the sob just comes out and I know he heard it.

"Now, Mercedes. Right now."

"Rave, please..."

"I know what it's like to not have anybody to talk to."

"You have your friend..."

"Who? Spider?"

"Yeah."

"Yeah... but Spider's a guy. A tech guy. You don't know these tech guys. To him, technology is his woman."

I laugh, feeling a little lighter in my heart.

"Really, he lives like a monk. He don't under-stand... certain things." Rave sighs.

I don't know why. It just came out.

"Okay. I'll meet you. Where?"

SHE'S BEAUTIFUL WHEN SHE'S crying. She

squints up her amazing eyes and kind of puckers up her pouty mouth. Her tears look like crystal drops pouring down her face. No wonder her father spoiled her. Every time he'd try to whup that little butt she'd squint up her eyes, pucker up her mouth, and he'd go all soft. If I had paternal instincts they'd be aroused right about now. My instincts are anything but.

"I'm sorry you had to go through that," I say. We're in her car again, in a parking lot. Alone. "Why'd you go there, though?"

"I wanted to find out more about him. He's attacking me, in my dreams. I can't sleep, Rave. I wanted to know who my attacker is."

"I told you who he is."

"Yeah... but... I wanted to know for myself. My father always says to know your enemy. Rave, I'm tired of other people directing my life. Fighting my battles. I wanna fight my own battles."

"Mercedes, I've known Shepherd all my life, and even I don't try to fight him myself. There are some enemies you can't... shouldn't confront head on by yourself. He's one."

"I got that," Mercedes says, sniffing a little. "But I'm glad I visited him."

"Oh? Why?"

"Because I got a feel for him. If I'm gonna fight him as you say, I have to know who I'm fighting, right?"

"Have you told... your husband yet?"

She doesn't say anything for a while, and I'm guessing she hasn't.

"Why not?" I ask.

"He's... he's not ready to hear that yet. You have to understand how he thinks about me. He and my father both. They think I'm some kind of trophy wife or something. It's how they think about women. Even my mother and D's mother, they are stay at home moms, who don't do nothing but shop and look pretty. I'm really starting to understand my mother, why she lives the way she does. It's because being married to my father put her in a box, like you said. And even though my mother-in-law tries to be social, she's in a box too. I mean, they're nice and everything, and I love them to death, but there's more to me than that."

She pouts her lovely lips, looking sad, and all I want to do is kiss them. I reach out and take her arms. She doesn't resist. I lean in a little closer, and then I pull her into a hug. I plant a kiss on her forehead and wipe away her tears.

"I admire your desire to fulfill your potential," I say, releasing her, "but are you ready to really face the world your husband and father inhabit? Are you ready to face Shepherd again?"

"No," Mercedes acknowledges. "He is dangerous. I know that now. But I'm my father's daughter, and my father was a member of The Brotherhood. I gotta do what I gotta do."

"Okay, so you need to know that we're not

aiming to kill Shepherd in the body. We killing him in the world of the spirit, and for that, you have to be very strong. He's gonna come at you with everything he's got, and it's not going to be easy."

"I know."

"It's important that you know your true identity. You're right when you say you're more than your father's daughter or your husband's wife. To Shepherd, you're much more than that. To him, you're a power he wants to use."

"I kinda get that, and kinda don't."

"You don't have to get it all. You just have to get the basics. I'll teach you the basics."

"What are the basics."

"The basics are when, where, and how."

She had gone very quiet.

"I heard what he said to you," I say, deciding to wade into the very deep waters we're already in.

"You did... how?"

"I heard him. He shouldn't have said those things. But that's how he is. He's very mean. That's his way of trying to break you. Break your confidence and spirit."

I lean towards her again, and turn her face to me. The way she looks at me, I know she feels about me the way I feel about her. I lean closer to her and kiss her on her lips. She closes her eyes. I take her in my arms and really kiss her, feeling her melt into me. It's a long kiss. She feels good in my arms. So sweet. Then she pushes me away.

"I... I can't do this," she says nervously. "I can't. I can't step out on D. I know we're having problems right now, but I love him and he loves me. He does."

She starts the car. "I gotta go," she says. "Get out."

"What?"

"Get out, Rave," she demands. "I can't be with you."

"But..."

"Please," she says. She looks truly afraid. "My life is already complicated enough. Please don't make it more complicated."

I open the door.

"I... I'll call you," she says, looking up at me as I close the door. "To get the basics. When, where, and how. I promise."

I look at her car as she drives away. I'll remember that kiss for the rest of my life.

Chapter Eighteen

Children Of The Brotherhood

"The children of the original Brotherhood are new and improved versions of their parents. Educated. Well-spoken. Polished by exposure to the advantages of wealth from the time they were born. And powerful. They don't know how much. Just thinking about them gives me goosebumps. How much I can achieve through them.

Isaiah's son is even more brilliant than he was. Dalvin's son even more furious than his father. As for Richard's son, there are no words to describe his kind of finely-tuned killer instinct. It's a rare gift. Adam's impetuous son is bolder than his father. And Ronnie's daughter is not only pure, but possesses strength she hasn't even begun to tap into. But she's Dalvin's wife now, and he'll put her through so much pain she'll have ample opportunity for self-discovery. Oh to have them together like the original Brotherhood—what a force I would have at my fingertips.

And I, The Shepherd would live forever in the beautiful, perfect body of Raven Stones. I can hardly wait..."

✡ ✡ ✡

It doesn't take me long to size up a man and know who I'm dealing with. Sometimes I can do it as soon as I lay eyes on him. His demeanor. The kind of clothes he wears. The way he wears them, the look on his face. Everything tells a story. The guy sitting in front of me is a playa. He got that ladies' man look. Everything is slick and in place. Hair pulled back in a ponytail, but his eyes are like hard black stones and I can see he's borderline evil. He and Spider sit next to each other like they buddies, probably for a long time, probably the way their fathers were.

"D, this Rave. Rave, this D," Spider introduces us.

"What up, Rave?" I say, the image of him walking through the restaurant with the old man fresh in my mind. And the way he looked at me, like he was trying to scoop out my soul. I push away the irritation I suddenly feel.

"How you doing, D?" he says. "Sorry for your loss, man."

"Thanks, so you a lawyer."

ACTUALLY, I'M AN ASSASSIN. A hit man. I moonlight as a lawyer. It's a cover. You know what I mean. You moonlight as a CEO, but you a killer too. You probably got as many hits under your belt as me. And I got plenty.

"Yes." I smile. "Corporate law."

"You work for the old man. Shepherd," D says, his eyes slicing through me. "The first time I saw you, you were with him."

"Yes, that's correct."

"You know him well?"

"Yeah. He was my guardian when I was a boy."

"Guardian?"

"When my father was killed, he... took care of my mother and me."

I can see him processing what I just said. "So... you probably know him better than anybody, then."

"Yeah. I know him real good."

"He's the one behind my father's death?" He leans back in his chair and closes his eyes. He looks like he's tuned out, but if my instincts are right—and they usually are—he's more alert than ever.

"Yes, he is."

"You know who actually shot him?" He opens his eyes, slowly, almost casually, and stares at me real cold.

Well, yes, as a matter of fact, I did. I took your daddy from you. And guess what macho man? I'm gonna take your wife, too.

He cocks his head. It's a slow, evil-looking movement, as if he'd heard my thoughts, though I know he didn't.

"The newspapers say he was killed by a man on a dirt bike, right?" I say.

"Yes, he was."

"Well, I hope the police find the guy soon." I nod.

"Oh, it don't matter if they find him," he says looking hard at me. "'Cause I will."

RAVE SMILES AT THAT, and for a moment, he seems like a regular, friendly kind of guy. I smile, too.

Spider is sitting next to him, his eyes glued to his tablet. He's typing fast with his stylus, looking like he ain't paying no attention to us at all.

What you doing over there, Spiderman? What are you writing? Who're you talking to? You playing me, man?

They say you can tell a man from the company he keeps. Now that I see Spider and this guy are buddies, I realize I can't trust Spider, at all. But I don't gotta trust him. I just have to work with him, for now. I'm even prepared to overlook the fact that I'd have to work with Jacob too, although I don't know if I can trust myself to be in the same room with him. That doesn't mean I forgive him for what he did to me. I don't forgive. It just means I'm allowing him to live for a short while longer. So when he swaggers into my office a few minutes later, I keep it real cool.

The good thing about having meetings on my turf is that everyone has to give up their weapons at the door. But I get to keep mine. It's sitting right next to me in my desk drawer, and all I need is an excuse to use it.

Please, Jacob. Give me an excuse to shoot you. It don't need to be a good one.

"Here's the thing, whatever's going down has to happen without my wife," I make clear.

Rave and Spider look at me, then at each other, then Rave looks at his hands and Spider looks at his tablet.

Rave nods slowly.

"I understand the reason for your decision," he says, "and I agree with it. Your wife is young, only eighteen, right? She doesn't need to get into that kind of thing so early. But..."

I knew it...

"...Just be sure it's her decision."

"It is." I stare Rave down before speaking again. "Just so you know, I don't like it when people question my decisions."

"Did I question your decision?" Rave asks.

"Yeah, you did."

He looks at me, eyes steady, face on ice. Then he smiles that cocky smile again.

Please give me an excuse to shoot you, Rave. Any little excuse will do.

Chapter Nineteen

Enter The Dark Side

Shepherd lives in a lavish spread in Lincoln Park. House three stories high, automatic gates. The place is riddled with cameras and there are suits everywhere. All day, there's traffic, food deliveries, medical deliveries with folks coming and going, conducting business. The place is like a compact version of Buckingham Palace.

I wasn't surprised when Rave told me Shepherd didn't trust him, and didn't let him in the room where he slept. Rave ain't someone you feel you could trust. He's cold and calculating and distant, even though he has a cool, friendly way about him, he gives off the vibe of living a double life. It's obvious he's crossed over to the dark side. He has all the unmistakable signs.

I don't trust Rave either. Ever since Ronnie

told me Shepherd had a special assassin working solo, I been wondering if Rave was that guy, if he was the killer who had the nerve to crash my wedding and murder my father.

I hold the image of the killer in my mind, and I think about Rave, his height, his build. He could be the guy. But I don't know for sure. Yet.

Ronnie and me staked out Shepherd's house for a long time. Spider linked us into the surveillance system inside the house and around the grounds outside. We watched everything from a wide screen monitor in Ronnie's office.

Ronnie was intense. His eyes never missed a thing. He knew how to read a situation better than anybody I knew except my father. I thought I was good, but next to this guy, I feel I'm just starting out all over again. I got to know his habits. If you wanna make him happy just keep him supplied with plenty of cigarettes and gallons of coffee.

"Ronnie, what do you think about all that stuff with the pentagram? Shepherd's oxygen chamber sits right in the middle of one. Does it really protect him like he thinks?"

"I think there is something to it," says Ronnie, slurping on his caramel macchiato. "And we should factor all that stuff in. We have one shot at Shepherd if we don't want him coming after us like the devil. We should use every bit of information we got."

So we planned our attack for the summer solstice, which ain't only the longest day of the year, it's also the time magicians can move between this world and the spirit world, according to Rave. Don't get it twisted. I don't believe in all that magic stuff. The only reason I'm going along with Rave is because it's a way to get to Shepherd.

THE EVENING OF JUNE Twentieth is warm and dry. Rave opens the door, and Ronnie and me slip inside. The house is huge. His ceiling alone must be about thirty feet high. Although it's summer, there's a chill in the foyer, and shadows weave in and out of each other in the gloom. There's definitely something creepy about the place.

Rave grips his Ruger with a silencer attached and me and Ronnie follow him up a broad, winding staircase. I got my Glock and Ronnie's got his Sig. Spider had disabled the main alarm and surveillance systems, but there's another set of cameras Shepherd controls from his room.

I get the weird feeling I'm being watched, and not by cameras either. I'm used to being watched by cameras. I feel there's someone right up behind me, looking over my shoulder. I look back and make them out in the shadows coming out of the hallway, silent as cats in the darkness. I swing round just as they materialize from the shadows. Rave and Ronnie and me raise our weapons and shoot, hardly making a sound in the eerily silent house. As they fall to the ground, I remember the bikers at my wedding, and know they would soon be pouring through every corridor and up the stairs. Shadow Walkers. That's what Rave called them. Trained assassins. Focused. Relentless. Suicidal. Unstoppable.

We run the rest of the way up the stairs, taking them two by two. Spider and Jacob are waiting for us. I can't believe my eyes when I see who else is there. Mercedes. Suited up like the rest of us. Her gun in her hand. I take a step towards her. Rave steps right up in front of me.

"Stay focused," he whispers, his eyes flashing fiercely at me.

I shove him, but he holds his ground.

"Mercy, why are you here?" I demand to know.

"Don't worry about me, D," she says in a low voice. "Really."

I stare at her, then at her father. He's as shocked as I am.

"We don't have all night," says Rave impatiently. "There are two other floors to go. Let's do this."

We take the stairs to the third floor. When we reach the top, we walk quickly along the long hallway. More Shadow Walkers come out of the darkness firing. We fire back. I feel the impact of a bullet in my vest and drop to the floor, hearing the bullets fly into the walls above me. I keep shooting, and I hear rather than see them fall to the ground.

I'm distracted. Mercedes is in this dangerous place, and I worry about her getting hurt. I look around for her. She's crouching next to Rave. I don't know if I should feel relieved or pissed. Spider runs ahead and kneels in front of a door, and I decide that the better I focus on what's going on, the better I can protect her. As we advance towards the door, I hear the soft click that means he'd popped the lock. We slip inside in single file.

The oxygen chamber looks bigger than in the photo. It's sitting in the center of the large pentagram, but it's empty. We look around. There's nothing in the room but the chamber. We scatter towards the adjoining rooms, each of us searching a room. I look in the old man's dressing room, carefully rifling through rows of expensive suits. Nothing. We converge into the main room again.

"Is there anywhere else he could be besides this room?" Jacob asks Rave.

"Yeah, the basement."

We follow him out the door, on the alert for more Shadow Walkers. The hallway is empty and quiet, too quiet. I remember Ronnie's words.

We run quickly down four flights of stairs to the basement. I take the controlled breaths I need to keep up my pace without getting winded now that I'm living with only half my lung capacity. I'll never forgive Jacob for that.

I feel a disturbing sensation of deja vu as I enter the basement, although I know I've never been down here before. It's large and well lit. And empty. A huge pentagram is engraved on the tiles in the

Ride Wit' Me Part 2

center of the room.

"Where is he, man?" I ask, feeling irritated and impatient.

Rave is standing, one leg supporting his weight, the other bent at a casual angle, his weapon in his hand. He looks at me. The moment of recognition is sudden and violent. I'm looking at my father's killer. His eyes lock into mine, and he smiles at me in the same mocking way he did at the restaurant. Involuntarily, I move towards him, my weapon raised. He turns to face me. Spider pushes himself in between the two of us.

"Guys," he says, "we don't have time for this now."

"You killed my father."

He don't say nothing, but the look in his eyes says it all. Slowly, he raises his gun and points it at me.

"Rave!" Mercy yells out. "What are you doing?"

So this is the way it's gonna play. I don't care if I go down in a hail of bullets. I'm gonna take Rave with me. Just then, the lights go out and the basement is suddenly pitch black and silent.

His voice penetrates the darkness, hoarse and rasping. His footsteps are slow, like he's taking a cool walk through the park.

"Hello, kids. I don't want you killing each other now. The party hasn't started yet. I got some real fun things planned for y'all."

I stand still in the darkness, the hand with my

gun following the sound of his footsteps. I'm so itching to squeeze the trigger.

Then I hear the sound. It's very familiar, though I don't remember ever hearing it before. It's disturbing, disorienting. I'm suddenly nauseated, and I feel I wanna pass out. I take a deep breath to steady myself. As the sound persists, my head spins as if I'm inhaling mind-altering fumes.

"Don't fight it," says Shepherd. "Thaaaat's right. Just go with it."

The sound doesn't get any louder, but it seems to get more intense. I fight to stay conscious. I get the strange sensation of my body going numb, while my mind swims somewhere out around me. I hear my gun hit the floor.

I realize the room ain't dark anymore, and that the light keeps getting brighter and brighter till I can see again. I'm alone in the basement. It's still and quiet. I look for my gun, but I don't see it. I walk quickly towards the steps and take them two by two to the top. When I open the door, a gust of wind hits me in the face. What the?

I step outside into the warm night, my heart pounding fast. I'm no longer in the city. There are no houses, no buildings, no streetlights, no streets. I'm in some kind of wide-open plain.

I hear the beating of wings. I look up and see the bird sailing, wings outstretched towards me. It's a huge black raven. The bird hovers in front of me, his black eyes piercing through me, his wings beating the air. Then he turns and flies in the direction he just came from. I feel he wants me to follow him, and I run after him, realizing that for the first time since I had been shot I'm not struggling to breathe. I have unlimited lung capacity and I run, faster and faster, enjoying the feeling of... freedom.

It seems as if the space around me is empty, as if there's nothing in it but me. I don't even get winded as I continue to run. I just run through unlimited space breathing unlimited air. It's the best feeling I ever had in my whole life.

I run until I come to a high chain fence and I can't go any further. The raven flies over the fence and I watch him glide into the sky until he disappears.

Chapter Twenty

Battling The Devil

I looked around. I'm in a courtyard made of raw concrete. There's a small house in the center and I walk towards it. I turn the knob on the door and go inside. A wooden pathway leads from the door into the house. I follow the pathway. It's long and seems to wind around and around and back on itself. I walk and walk and walk.

Finally, I come to an empty room. There's a man sitting cross-legged on the floor. His head is bowed, and he's wrapped up in a huge gray shawl which covers him from his head to his feet. I stand still for a moment, watching him. He raises his head and throws off the shawl. It's Shepherd.

He isn't wearing his eye patch, and he looks at me out of one eye. The other eye socket is empty. Without thinking, I walk towards him. Suddenly, it occurs to me that he wants me to walk into him. I stop. He raises his hand and beckons to me and I take another step towards him. Something inside tells me that I don't want to be swallowed up by him. I stop walking.

The old man smiles. His eye is piercing, but I've made up my mind that I'm not going to let him consume me. I hold my ground. He shakes his head as if he thinks I'm being a bad boy and disappears.

Then I feel as if I'm being overpowered by someone or something I can't see. I swing out, not connecting to anything, but I feel its strength. It's bigger than me, and much, much stronger.

I have been fighting all my life, and I've never let a man get the better of me, no matter how big or strong he is. I know how to beat down men twice my size, but this opponent has no physical size. I couldn't connect with him. This is a different kind of battle. It's a battle of the soul, a battle of wills.

I feel like I'm suffocating, like I can't breath, but I keep on resisting him. He's all over me. I can feel him trying to crush me, squeeze my life out of me, and for the first time in my life I feel fear. I fear the beast that's trying to devour me, and I fear the fear I'm feeling. But I know that if I give in even a little, I'm finished. I set my mind to keep on resisting. Even to the point of annihilation.

The beast is beating me down, and my mind says there's no way I'm gonna beat him. He's too strong, but my inside says I have to try.

Then he eases up off me a little, and I'm able to breathe again. But it isn't over. He's coming back. I know it.

When you're fighting for your life, you grab at anything. I know I can't continue to fight the beast head-on. I need something else, some kind of back up.

The memory comes like a tiny bubble that blows itself up and breaks. But I hold on to it. It's the memory of a dream I been having for a long time. It comes again like a small pinpoint of light.

In the dream, I'm in a church, standing just inside the door. There's a coffin in the aisle and the folks inside are singing a funeral song and making symbols in the air with their fingers. I don't know who's in the coffin, but I go over to one of the pews and stand beside a man. I crane my neck to see the coffin over the heads of the people in front of me.

"Fire," he says.

"Excuse me?" I say, still trying to see the coffin.

"You need a sign," says the man. "Fire is your sign."

"Yeah," I say and laugh, "we'll burn his house down good."

"I'm not talking about that," he says. "I'm talking about your symbol. You have to learn how to make it."

And that was it. That was the entire dream. I realize I had been dreaming it for a long time and never remembered it.

The triangle. That was the symbol for fire. As I think about it, I see it take form in my mind. But I'm tired, and I'm in a panic because I know the beast is going to come back soon. I try to hold the shape in my mind. It floats in and out of my thoughts, awkward, incomplete.

The beast comes again so suddenly I'm not ready for him. He has a large, bulky coiling kind of presence, like a huge snake or dragon. He moves in on me, and I feel like I'm drowning in my fear and hatred, but it's my hatred for him that seems to help me keep on resisting him. I can't think. The three lines of the triangle are all over the place. I force my mind to bring them together. But I'm so wasted I can't. I fall on the ground, and the beast throws himself on me, pressing down on me, squeezing the breath out of me. I fall into a thick, deep darkness. I can't move. Can't breathe.

So THIS IS WHAT it's like to die. This is what death is like. There ain't no bright lights, no singing angels. Death is dark and cold and merciless and sudden. Death pounces on you when you're not expecting it. It devours you when you're alone.

The darkness around me feels like a grave. It presses in on me. I'm terrified like I've never been. I feel I'm going crazy in that tight, dark space. It's the kind of wild desperation that makes me want to scream like a little kid, tear away at the darkness, claw my way out of it. I can't move. Can't open my mouth. I hear myself scream deep inside, a raw sound that rips through my soul.

I don't know how long I screamed like that. The sensation of being suffocated is so bad, my heart seems ready to pop outta my chest. That's when I went very still. I had run out of air and all I could do is lie still and wait to die. And in the hush of those final seconds before death, I think of her. Mercy. My sweet, Mercy.

I love her so much. I wonder where she is. Did she battle the beast, too? Is she feeling this? Is she dying this horrible death? No. Oh no, no. I can't bear to think of her going through this and my father. Did he scream in the excruciating fear of his own powerlessness, like me? Man, I wouldn't wish this on my worse enemy. Not even Jacob who tried to kill me. Not even Raven, who killed my father.

How many men had I sent to their graves? Did they squirm like worms crying out in the darkness of their souls in those awful final moments before annihilation? And for what? What was the point of it all? What did I gain from it? Some fleeting sense of power? It all seems so senseless now that if I could take all of it back I would. I really would. Because I know now I have no power.

Then I feel that I'm not alone anymore. It isn't that there's someone else with me in my grave. It's more like there's a presence someplace around. I feel a small jolt of hope, as if a small pinpoint of light had come on in the pitch blackness, and I see them like faint lights in my mind's eye. The three lines of the triangle.

They float in front my eyes, bouncing around in their own space until they touch. They light up brighter as they come together. Then the triangle bursts into flames and sits in a blazing inferno above me. I feel light as a feather, and I'm no longer imprisoned by the darkness. I rise up towards the flames and walk through the fire into the middle of the burning lines. The flames feel cool. They don't burn me at all.

I hear the fire blaze loud and high all around me. I hear the sound of furious, crashing waves. I hear a rumbling like the sound of an earthquake, and the sound of a violent rushing wind. It was a furious storm, as I wonder if the world is coming to an end. I hold my ground as the fury of the storm gets stronger.

Then I see the pentagram, its lines meeting in five points lit up, the symbols of the five elements appearing one by one on each point, and I knew that we had all made it. I feel strong, as if I have un-limited power, but it's not only my power. It's the power of all of us combined. It's the power of The Brotherhood.

The old man's face appears suddenly above the pentagram, like a death head, and I know the power of The Brotherhood is stronger than he is. He knows it too, and man does that make him mad. He screams and howls, but there's nothing he can do. Then he disappears as if the elements of the storm had snuffed him out.

Then suddenly, I'm back in the basement. The place is shaking like there's an earthquake. Huge flames are shooting up from the floor, bouncing off the walls. Water is gushing along the floor and there's a wind blowing that's so strong it almost knocks me off my feet. I see Spider, Rave, Jacob, and Mercedes.

"Get out quick," Rave yells.

We take the stairs. Then we reach the outside of the house just as it explodes. I'm thrown forward by the force of the explosion. I fall on the sidewalk and roll forward. I lie on my back winded. The sky is red from the flames. I heard the sound of running feet just before I black out.

Chapter Twenty-One

Together Forever At Last

I woke up in my condo. When I opened my eyes, the first thing I see is Mercedes sitting on the side of the bed.

"D?" she whispers. "You okay?"

"Mercedes," I mouthed, feeling beyond happy to see her to the point I wanna cry. I take her little head in my hands and pull her close to me and kiss her hard.

"Mercedes," I said, pulling back a little. "Did everybody make it out of the house?"

"Yeah, they all did."

"Where's your dad?" I ask.

"He's out front, in the living room, waiting for you to wake up. He found you on the sidewalk passed out and brought us here. He said if you didn't wake up soon, we'd take you to the hospital.

You sure you feel alright?"

"Yeah, baby. I'm okay." Then I remembered. I sit up in the bed. "Mercy! Did you feel it? The power of The Brotherhood?"

"Oh. My. Goodness," she breathes.

"It was awesome!" I said, reliving the rush I got from the experience.

"Wasn't it?" she agrees.

"That sort of power, Mercy. Raw, naked power."

She looks into my eyes. Fearlessly.

"Mercy," I say, feeling that I can talk to her about what's on my mind at that moment. "Spider told me the pentagram can either stand for conflict or harmony. Or both. But when we all stood on the points, I felt we connected."

She nods. "We did connect, D. But we needed to in order to destroy Shepherd."

"I've got some unresolved conflict with those guys, Jacob, Rave, and even Spider, 'cause he played me."

"Yeah," she says, "I know."

"Usually everything is so black and white to me, but after what happened, everything seems more... complex than before. It's unfinished business. Like a loose end I don't know how to get rid of, but I know needs to be dealt with."

"I get you, but you know what, D? You don't have to tackle that conflict right now, or that loose end. It might play out different from how you expect it to."

"Yeah, I guess so, but one thing I'm sure of is Jacob will be dealt with, but not before Rave. He's now at the top of my list. He took away my father. The only man I've ever loved and for that he will be dealt with. Maybe not at this moment, but it will happen. That's a promise."

"I know, D. But right now I'm just happy we survived Shepherd. I feel what we went through has made our love and bond stronger than ever."

"You right, baby," I said, lying back on the pillow and pulling her down with me. We lie close together, holding each other. She's precious, oh so precious to me. I never want to let her go. "We have a little unfinished business of our own."

"What's that?"

"Our honeymoon."

"Oh." She smiles. "I know you have a lot of business you need to handle, D. We don't have to do that now. I'm starting to understand that marriage is about compromising. So I can wait."

"No, Mercy, you've waited long enough. Don't you want us to go on a honeymoon?"

"Of course," she beams. "I really, really do. But if you're busy..."

"So let's do it. No more excuses."

She's suddenly excited. "You mean it!" She smiles in that special way that touches the core of my heart.

"I do. Remember how we said we'd go to the Caribbean?"

"Oh wow! Yeah."

"Where do you wanna go? Jamaica? Aruba?"

"Oh D, let's go to Barbados."

"Wanna go to Barbados, huh?"

"Yes, I do."

"So Barbados it is. We'll leave tomorrow."

"That soon? We gotta do so many things before we leave."

"Like what?"

"Like pack..."

"We don't have to pack. We'll pick up some swimsuits and clothes when we get there. We can leave first thing in the morning. As soon as we get up."

"Barbados. Wow! I can hardly wait."

"Mercy," I say, taking her face in my hands. "I love you, baby. I love you with everything that's in me. And I always will."

She smiles her beautiful smile at me. "I love you too, D. With all my heart... forever and always."

Chapter Twenty-Two

Change Is Good

When the house explodes in a blaze of fire, so does my life as Rave. Its momentum throws me ten feet forward. Then I'm up on my feet and running.

I feel an unfamiliar exhilaration as I run through the night, my sneakers pounding the sidewalk. With the old man gone, everything's gonna change. But you know what, change is good.

That night, for the first time in years, I slept like a baby. I sold my cars and my house, and moved into a shabby little apartment in the projects, 'cause I wanted to get rid of everything associated with my old life. For the first two weeks, I didn't go outside, just sat in the darkness of my room, enjoying my hard-won freedom. The walls in my apartment are thin, and the lives of the folks who live around me filter through into my little world. I hear them fighting. I hear them making up, making babies. Life is good. My only regret is that Mercedes isn't here to share it with me. But life is also mysterious. I know I'll see her again one day.

I've been a Shadow Walker for a long time. I've walked between this world and the spirit world. I don't only know how to kill a man's body. I can snuff out his soul as well. Shepherd is dead because I taught the sons and daughter of The Brotherhood how to kill him. Shepherd gave them the nightmares that turned them against each other. I gave them the tools they needed to fight him. I gave them the knowledge of the symbols that identify them in the spirit world so they could call for back up when they needed it. And when they felt they were spent and wasted and dying, I walked into their darkness and led them out.

The first time I killed a man I was ten years old. I've taken down hundreds of men since then. Dalvin Dewitt was the last. But I know that the time has come to walk a different path. Thing is, I haven't decided what that path is. This is why I'm not going after Dalvin, though I know him well enough to know he's not going to forgive me for killing his old man.

The first day I stepped outside my apartment, I was pleasantly warmed by the light of the sun. It's fall, and there's a chill in the air. I pull my hoodie over my head, stick my hands in my pockets and hop down the steps. There's a pile of black garbage bags on the curb and dog poo in the middle of the sidewalk. A group of kids pass in front of me, talking loudly of very profane things. I smile. I wanted to enjoy my new life, if only for a short span of time.

I know Dalvin will follow me even here. I wouldn't expect less of him. He's a true son of The Brotherhood. He may show up in the middle of the night. I may turn a corner and he'll be there, his gun pointed at my chest. No biggie. I'm ready because it's not if but when... because he will come... guns blazing.

Order Form
A King Production
P.O. Box 912
Collierville, TN 38027
www.joydejaking.com
www.twitter.com/joydejaking

Name: _____

Address: _____

City/State: _____

Zip: _____

QUANTITY	TITLES	PRICE	TOTAL
_____	Bitch	$15.00	_____
_____	Bitch Reloaded	$15.00	_____
_____	The Bitch Is Back	$15.00	_____
_____	Queen Bitch	$15.00	_____
_____	Last Bitch Standing	$15.00	_____
_____	Superstar	$15.00	_____
_____	Ride Wit' Me	$12.00	_____
_____	Ride Wit' Me Part 2	$12.00	_____
_____	Stackin' Paper	$15.00	_____
_____	Trife Life To Lavish	$15.00	_____
_____	Trife Life To Lavish II	$15.00	_____
_____	Stackin' Paper II	$15.00	_____
_____	Rich or Famous	$15.00	_____
_____	Rich or Famous Part 2	$15.00	_____
_____	Rich or Famous Part 3	$15.00	_____
_____	Bitch A New Beginning	$15.00	_____
_____	Mafia Princess Part 1	$15.00	_____
_____	Mafia Princess Part 2	$15.00	_____
_____	Mafia Princess Part 3	$15.00	_____
_____	Mafia Princess Part 4	$15.00	_____
_____	Mafia Princess Part 5	$15.00	_____
_____	Boss Bitch	$15.00	_____
_____	Baller Bitches Vol. 1	$15.00	_____
_____	Baller Bitches Vol. 2	$15.00	_____
_____	Baller Bitches Vol. 3	$15.00	_____
_____	Bad Bitch	$15.00	_____
_____	Still The Baddest Bitch	$15.00	_____
_____	Power	$15.00	_____
_____	Power Part 2	$15.00	_____
_____	Drake	$15.00	_____
_____	Drake Part 2	$15.00	_____
_____	Female Hustler	$15.00	_____
_____	Princess Fever "Birthday Bash"	$9.99	_____
_____	Nico Carter The Men Of The Bitch Series	$15.00	_____

Shipping/Handling (Via Priority Mail) $6.50 1-2 Books, $8.95 3-4 Books add $1.95 for ea. Additional book.

Total: $_____ **FORMS OF ACCEPTED PAYMENTS:** Certified or government issued checks and money Orders, all mail in orders take 5-7 Business days to be delivered